W9-CEU-367

DISCARD

SOMETHING WATCHING ME

KENDRA HADNOTT

Something Watching Me
Copyright © 2015 by Kendra Hadnott All rights reserved.
First Print Edition: January 2015
ISBN 13: 978-0-9909638-0-6
ISBN 10: 0-9909638-0-2

Cover and Formatting: Streetlight Graphics

Publishing: Miles Way Press

No part of this book may be reproduced, scanned, or distributed in any printed or electronic form without permission. Please do not participate in or encourage piracy of copyrighted materials in violation of the author's rights. Thank you for respecting the hard work of this author.

This is a work of fiction. Names, characters, places, and incidents either are the product of the author's imagination or are used fictitiously, and any resemblance to locales, events, business establishments, or actual persons—living or dead—is entirely coincidental.

R0444080436

DEDICATION

To Eric, Debra, Debbie, and the Muhammads

—

CHAPTER 1

"**D**on't just sit there!" yelled Mark.

"They'll kill me if I run around the corner. Do you want me to die or what?" Stephen said.

"We're going to die just sitting here, anyway. We'll be right beside you. C'mon, man. It took us so long to get here. Don't chicken out on us now."

"I'm far from a chicken. I'm the only reason we made it this far. Did you forget that?" asked Stephen.

Mark and Vince didn't answer. Instead they moved closer to the street corner with slow, careful movements.

"Out of my way," Stephen said, quietly pushing past Mark and Vince. Who did they think they were? He crouched low as he inched closer to the dingy, brownish brick wall. He could see nothing around him but bushes with blurry blocks of green and gray sidewalks peppered with soda cans and paper.

"I'm going in," Stephen affirmed to his friend Vince through his earpiece.

"Here it comes!"

"I know, I know," Stephen said impatiently. He felt a nervous tickle as if an invisible finger were sliding down his arm. He still dreaded hearing those words. He moved forward, easing toward the sharp corner of the brick wall.

"What's taking you so long, man? Go!"

"Look, man, I can't concentrate. Just be quiet for a second," Stephen said to Mark and Vince. He rubbed his hand against his pant leg. Something about what was coming next unnerved him.

"He's not gonna do it anyway. He's just gonna start talking about ghosts again," Mark teased. Stephen heard Vince laugh.

"I never said ghosts. I said...Look, whatever. I'm not paying attention to you. I *am* gonna do it. Just shut up and let me do it," Stephen said, annoyed. Every part of his body felt frozen, but still he cautiously inched closer to the wall's edge and turned the corner. His hands shook. He knew what was around that corner.

"Holy cow, he did it."

Stephen blushed as his hands continued to tremble. *This* was the part that he hated: the waiting. Thinking about what stared him down as he stood on the corner, idle and dumbfounded.

"Stephen!" his father yelled, startling him. The video game controller dropped from Stephen's hands and thudded on the wooden floor. He stared all around his room from his sloppily made bed to the basketball and football posters splashed against the wall around his closet. Nothing looked out of the ordinary, for today at least. His bedroom door cracked open.

"Hey, sport. You gettin' ready?" Stephen's father said, peeking his head inside.

"Yeah. Yeah, Dad. Almost ready," he said, ripping off his gaming earpiece and wiping his hands on his pants again. His scalp felt wet and cool with sweat.

"Good, because I would hate to have to explain to McGruder that the zombie ambush kept us from attending this afternoon," his father said, smiling. He nodded his head toward the video game and TV. "You get past the zombies yet?" he asked.

"Not yet," Stephen said.

"Okay. Maybe some of the other kids in the neighborhood have played *Dead Zombie Attack,*" he said casually.

Stephen knew what his father was getting at and it wasn't going to happen—not if it was up to the other kids, anyway. "Probably not, though," said Stephen. He glanced at his video game character, who was by now getting eaten by a pack of moaning, drooling zombies. Stephen was glad that he couldn't hear Mark and Vince, though he was sure that he'd hear more than enough taunting after he got back from the town meeting.

"Okay, well, I'll be downstairs, sport. Grab whatever you have to and lets go." He ducked his head out of the door and shut it abruptly.

"I'm coming!" Stephen replied through the closed door. He stood on top of his bed, his small feet barely making a dent in the mattress, and eyed his basketball cards—the good ones that might've been worth something. The ones that other kids might have wanted to see. He decided against it. Between Vince and Mark, he already had friends. Who needed other people when you had friends *and* video games?

He hopped from his bed and raced downstairs.

"Whoa. Careful," his father said as Stephen nearly knocked him over at the bottom of the stairwell. His father fixed his plain black tie and straightened his cufflinks. "How do I look? Am I together?" Stephen's father asked him, standing strong and rigid like a stone.

"Of course. You're *my* dad. You get your looks from me," Stephen answered.

His father smiled and playfully rubbed the top of Stephen's head. "Let's go," he said, spiking Stephen's gelled black hair back into place. "Matt, let's go!" his father yelled up the stairs, fixing his tie again.

A tall, chubby Matt came rushing down the stairs, each thud of his size thirteen sneakers sounding heavier than the next. People often thought Matt was older than his age...until he opened his mouth.

"Nice hairdo, grass head," Matt said, running his fingers over Stephen's spiky hair. "It even makes you look a little taller."

——✳——✳——✳——✳——✳——

The ride to the town meeting was silent. Stephen's father gripped the steering wheel tightly, looking at himself in the mirror every so often to adjust his tie and fix his hair. Matt was texting someone who was likely as lame as he was. And Stephen waited with excitement and anticipation to ride past the McCallister house, which he'd heard had been a homeless shelter years ago.

He could have sworn that there was something just beyond the McCallister house's broken window—*something* watching him. The first time he saw it, he swore it was only a piece of gunk stuck stubbornly to the corner of his eye. The second time, he was sure it was just his reflection. The third time, he concluded it was a hallucination from playing *Dead Zombie Attack Part V* for ten consecutive hours. By the fourth time, he began to suspect something or someone lived beyond the McCallister house's boarded doorway.

Stephen wished he could share his belief with someone. During a *Dead Zombie Attack V* night, Stephen had tried telling Vince and Mark about what watched him at the McCallister house, but they were skeptical. "You feel okay?" Vince had asked. "Right," Mark had said with criticism in his voice. But there was no denying the things that lived inside of the McCallister house, and no one but Stephen ever seemed to notice the gloomy pair of eyes that stared out the window every time he passed by.

Chills surged through Stephen as his dad's car drove past the McCallister house now. Even from far away, the faded reddish brown brick gave away the house's true age. As he got closer, he studied the window—the same rectangular window where something watched him through jagged shards of glass. He pressed his face against the car window, eager to get a better look.

But this time he saw nothing: the McCallister house's window was black and bare. He slumped back in his seat, awaiting the boredom that was the town meeting.

Stephen's father got to the town meeting faster than they ever had. He parked and scrambled out of the car, asking his usual set of questions:

"Tie straight?" he asked, adjusting it a final time and holding his hands away from it.

"Yes, Dad."

"Good." He rushed to put his black suit jacket on and buttoned it. "How am I looking?"

"Handsome like your son," Stephen replied as he always did.

"You wish," Matt mumbled underneath his breath.

"You are your father's children," he said, putting his arms around Matt and Stephen. "I'll catch up with you two after the meeting. Wait for me by the door."

Stephen's father rushed into the old warehouse. The same warehouse where children sat and listened attentively at town meetings as though their lives depended on it. Some kids didn't have to go. Stephen hadn't been so lucky. His mother and father like many other Wally Heights parents wanted their children to be *informed* and *politically aware*...whatever that meant. His stomach dropped as he thought about the slow, deep drag in the mayor's voice. *'Here we go again,'* Stephen thought, mentally preparing himself.

The town meeting was crowded as usual. Stephen watched as his father took his place on stage behind the podium. The four security guards standing below and in front of the stage looked stern with their tense faces and hands crossed in front of them. All of McGruder's staff had been so loyal and stoic in the wake of McGruder's divorce scandal in Illinois, and even now, here they all stood, proud and alert, ready to take a bullet for a man that so many people back in Illinois hated.

Stephen sat in a cold, metal chair toward the back of the room. Matt sat down and scooted a seat away from Stephen. A hush fell over the room. Stephen's father cleared his throat before his voice boomed into the microphone. "Thank you all for being here. Without further ado, I want to bring to the podium—Mayor McGruder."

Everyone stood in silence, waiting on the mayor. Someone's cough echoed throughout the warehouse. The security guards in the front of the room looked even more stern-faced than they had before—sturdy and still. As Mayor McGruder, a chubby man in a loose-fitting suit and a funny-looking comb-over, walked through an open, dark doorway and on stage, everyone immediately took their seats. Stephen watched as Mayor McGruder squared up to the podium, his stubby hands grabbing the sides.

"Good evening, Wally Heights," Mayor McGruder started. *Generic.* "Thank you for coming out. There are many things that you could be doing right now, but you're—"

Here with me, Stephen thought, finishing the mayor's sentence. Almost nothing that came out of *Mayor* McGruder's mouth was original—a stark contrast from McGruder's days in Illinois as a reverend. *Reverend* McGruder, who preached back in Illinois, had been loved, respected, and admired. That is, until the divorce thing happened with Mrs. McGruder—which Stephen guessed had been a horrendously bad thing. McGruder had left Illinois altogether and decided to become a mayor—that was when all of the trouble started.

McGruder had offered Stephen's father, a faithful supporter of the church, a chief-of-staff position, and Stephen's father had jumped at the chance quicker than he had ever jumped at anything before. Stephen had been excited too. Not many kids could say that their father was involved in politics. It would be a good thing for everyone, Stephen had concluded. Until he found out that he would be moving.

"Come on, it'll be fun. A new beginning, a chance to meet new people, a free mortgage, the possibility of running for mayor once McGruder's term is up... Who knows where this might lead?" Dad had said with excitement in his voice. Now Stephen wished he had told his father that money and mortgages and new beginnings didn't matter.

Stephen felt a pang of nostalgia. He wished he were with his mother on her business trip back in Hinsdale, Illinois—even if it did mean sitting through a bunch of boring work meetings about insurance. At least then, he could visit Vince and Mark. A bunch of kids who listened in meetings, a mysterious house that no one but him knew was haunted, no going over Vince's or Mark's house for *Dead Zombie Attack* marathons—Stephen hardly thought the move to Wally Heights, Alabama, was worth it.

Stephen yawned and used the back of his hand to wipe the tears from his eyes. Another result of a sleepless *Dead Zombie Attack Part V* night. There was nothing more frustrating than having his McCallister house high crushed by the drab sight of rows of chairs and an ugly wooden podium. Stephen covered his nose from the musty, stuffy smell of the town meeting warehouse.

"What about the McCallister house for a meeting place?" Stephen heard someone say, interrupting his thoughts. "The old abandoned place on Fifteenth and Lowe. It's about the only large, empty building we've got left in this town anyway." Stephen sat a little straighter and looked around for the voice. He had heard something in the last town meeting about plans to make the town meeting warehouse into a grocery store, but he had never thought that anyone would suggest meeting at the McCallister house instead.

"The McCallister house. Right. I suppose we can fix it up a little. All in favor of the McCallister house say aye," said the mayor.

Excitement began to swell in Stephen. He could hardly keep his legs from bouncing. Maybe he'd have someone to explore the McCallister house with after all.

"Aye," some people in the crowd said.

"Well, seems like that'll be our only choice right about now. If no one has any objections, McCallister house it is."

The room was silent enough to hear a blink.

The mayor cleared his throat. The sound rang fiercely in the quiet, crowded room. "Next order of business: announcements." He cleared his throat again. "Crill's store is going to buytheslkdlksgkslj..."

The mayor's words seemed to meld together, making everything sound like one long, incomprehensible word. Yawning again, Stephen glanced over to a long, slender leaking pipe. He cut his yawn short, but his mouth remained open and his eyes watered just the same.

Just beyond the pipe and not far from where the mayor spoke was a headless, bodiless, and familiar pair of eyes. They jerked around anxiously as though they were searching for something. Stephen studied the eyes closer as a wave of heat and dizziness overtook him. He thought to dart out of the room, but shock weighed him down. Was he really looking at a ghost? Was this the *thing* that had been watching him? His screams clung nervously to the back of his throat.

Stephen gaped in fear as the eyes rolled every which way. For a moment, they settled on staring in the direction opposite him before they began to jerk again. A girl screamed loudly, interrupting Mayor McGruder's monotone town announcements. The scream sent another surge of fear through Stephen.

The mayor paused and grabbed the sides of his suit jacket. He stared into the audience curiously, while one of the burly security men rushed to the girl and escorted her out. Grateful to have a distraction, Stephen watched the man as he gently guided her out of the room. He could see the girl shaking even from where he sat.

When Stephen looked at her face closely, he recognized her. The girl next door...literally. He sat still, careful not to bring any attention to himself.

A couple of girls sitting to the far right stared at the screaming girl and giggled softly. The eyes sitting idly by the pipe stopped jerking and stared directly at Stephen.

CHAPTER 2

Although Stephen hadn't seemed to notice, Wendy Foxhill had studied him carefully at the town meeting earlier that day. Wendy lay on her bed as she shuffled her basketball cards in her hands. For the past few hours, she had tried desperately to drown out the day's events.

Earlier in the town meeting, something had stared at Wendy intensely—a set of eyes that only stopped glaring at her when she screamed. She had frantically turned to Grandpa Lou, but he didn't seem to notice it, since he was already halfway asleep. And what was even stranger was that no screams followed hers. She wondered why no one else had been as scared as she was. The mayor still stood proudly at the podium, the crowd still looked up at him with glazed eyes, and a few of the other girls at the meeting had laughed at her as security escorted her out— it was business as usual for everyone else.

Wendy remembered waiting with her

grandfather on the lonely, littered bus stop in front of the McCallister House right before the meeting. She had never quite trusted that house. There always seemed to be things moving through the darkness, and she had always felt something gazing at her through the windows.

Wendy tossed her basketball cards to the side. They no longer distracted her. By now, her room had grown cluttered with handballs, baseballs, basketballs, specimen samples from her microscope kit, and arts and crafts books. If Grandpa Lou hadn't forbid her to play with her loud toys in the basement, this would be the perfect time to do so. But Grandpa Lou had made it clear that she wasn't to go anywhere near the basement since the steps, he said, were unsafe. And with the unsettling sounds Wendy had heard coming through the basement door, she vowed never to ask Grandpa Lou why he hadn't bothered to get them fixed. Still, none of that stopped her from wanting to beat on the bass drum tucked away in the basement until her thoughts became nothing more than a series of loud thumps.

Her mind went back to the image of the eyes at the town meeting. She couldn't forget that gaze, the way the eyes floated, the way they twitched until they found her. They were starting to appear closer to her than they ever had before.

Wendy glanced out of her bedroom window, hoping to find the same mundane sights that she always saw. She was instantly comforted by the brownish grass in her yard that Grandpa Lou had stopped tending to and the rows of big, reaching trees that guarded the sidewalk in front of each house.

She backed away from the window, noticing the familiar stretch of dead trees that led to the McCallister house. Next month's town meeting would be held at the McCallister house—the place where the eyes seemed to live. A knot formed in Wendy's stomach.

She turned from the gray, rainy haze outside of her window to the inside of her brightly lit bedroom. The smiling stuffed animals in her closet stared at her. They had always felt like her protectors, even when the staring eyes frightened her. But today, even their still gaze sent a chill through her.

Wendy walked over to her bedroom closet and shut the door. Being watched by anything or anyone was too much to handle right now. No place felt safe. She thumped down the stairs, hoping the sound would wake her grandfather. Something inside her itched to know what watched her, but she was sure that she couldn't handle finding out. Not right now, anyway. She couldn't be alone any longer.

But as usual, Grandpa Lou proved to be nearly impossible to wake. She walked into the kitchen and tried to stomp on a spider skittering about, staring in Grandpa Lou's direction as she did. No luck.

Wendy swung the dingy white refrigerator door open. A jar of olives crashed to the floor. She stared for a while at the green oval olives with red dots on the end. They seemed to stare back at her, patiently waiting to be cleaned up.

"What did you do in here?" She heard her grandpa's groggy voice as he walked through the doorway into the kitchen. "You've been acting uptight since this morning. What's the matter with you?" he asked.

How would you know? You've been asleep this entire time, Wendy thought. "Nothing," she said instead. "I'm just tired." She dared not tell Grandpa or any other adult about the eyes she saw at the town meeting. They would only judge her.

"Well, pick these up," Grandpa Lou said, pointing at the olives. "You just gonna stand there and look at 'em? Pick 'em up! Perfectly good jar of olives. Wasted. Unbelievable."

Wendy lethargically grabbed a paper towel and bent down to wipe the juice from the olives. "I didn't do it on purpose," she mumbled.

"What?" asked Grandpa Lou. Wendy had almost asked the same question of herself. Rarely had she spoken back to an adult, especially Grandpa Lou.

Wendy didn't know what to say. She focused on wiping the juice from the floor. Her hand shook a little as she moved the towel back and forth.

"What are you good for? Making messes and cleaning them. That's what," muttered her grandpa as he walked out of the kitchen.

Wendy turned red as she threw the paper towel on the floor. She stormed out of the kitchen and past Grandpa Lou with tears in her eyes without saying a word. She put on her gym shoes, not bothering to lace them, and opened the front door.

"You'll be back!" Wendy heard her grandpa yell as she slammed the door behind her. She stormed off into the cool evening air, praying that she was alone.

CHAPTER 3

"Y ou saw the inside of the McCallister house?" Stephen asked, as he inched closer to his father.

"Yes, I did," his father said. He squinted harder at the poster-sized paper as though he could tune Stephen out with his eyes. "Why do you care?" his father asked.

"Huh?" said Stephen. He hadn't been prepared for questions; he just needed answers.

"I said," his father started as he marked an "X" by one of the doors on the drawing, "why do you care? What's so fascinating about the McCallister house?"

"Nothing," Stephen said quickly. "Whoa, is that the floor plan to the McCallister house?" Stephen asked, pointing at the drawing that his father stared at.

"You're worrying me, kiddo."

"Well, what did you see? Why did you go there?" Stephen asked eagerly. If he could only find out what was inside.

Stephen's father looked up from his drawing and studied Stephen. "This is someplace new for the mayor. Always good to know your surroundings."

"What did it look like?"

"A house. An old one."

"That's it?"

"That's it," his father confirmed.

Stephen bowed his head, confused and disappointed all at once. Why did the eyes that watched him so passionately through the window not watch his father? Had he seen the eyes and just chosen to not tell Stephen?

"Hey, sport. Why don't you go play the game? I bet Vince and Mark miss you. Or how about going outside? There are plenty of kids in this neighborhood. I haven't seen you go outside yet," said Stephen's father.

"They're all lame," Stephen said, slouching in a chair next to his father.

"Everyone can't be lame."

"Wanna bet?" Stephen asked sarcastically.

"Try. I know it's been tough being the only new family in town, but just try to make friends. At least try."

"I already have friends," Stephen said defiantly. *Besides,* Stephen thought, *this is your fault anyway. You took me from the only friends I had.*

"Friends that live in the same state, maybe?" Stephen's father asked, oblivious.

"I have friends, Dad. Thanks anyway."

Stephen went in his room and put on his gaming headphones. He had no time to focus on new friends and his father's selfishness. He was here in Wally Heights now and that was it.

Stephen thought over the conversation that he just had with his father. Had his dad lied to him? If not, why couldn't his dad see the things he saw? It was all too much for now. It was time to unwind. He turned on his headphones and continued his zombie game.

"Stephen here, where are you guys?" he said, speaking into the headset.

"I'm here. Vince is on his way over," Mark said.

"Oh, okay." Stephen hoped that Mark couldn't hear the jealousy in his voice. Once upon a time, *he* would've been the one on his way to Mark's house.

"Where've you been? We've been waiting on you to beat this level all day. We're right at the part where the zombies drop from the sky," Mark said excitedly.

"I've been busy, I guess," Stephen said, holding the game controller loosely.

"More ghost stories?"

"Yes, but you wouldn't believe me anyway if I told you."

"Where were they this time?"

"They followed me to the town meeting.

They just hovered there and watched. I don't know. It was weird."

"What town meeting?" Mark asked.

"McGruder's. He's a mayor down here now. He's pretty bad at it too," Stephen said chuckling.

"Reverend McGruder as a mayor...there are some things that I will just never understand." Mark paused before he spoke again. "What about these ghosts?" he asked curiously.

"I don't know if they're ghosts. They're just eyes. They don't do anything. They just keep watching. Pretty sure they live in that old abandoned house I've been telling you about," Stephen answered.

"The McCallister house?"

"You actually listen? Maybe you aren't such a jerk after all, man," Stephen teased.

"Whatever. Look, if they keep watching and they're—hold on. Doorbell. I think Vince is here," he said, interrupting himself.

Minutes later, Mark picked up where he left off as if he had never stopped. "If they're following you, why don't you flip the script? Follow them. Might as well find out what the deal is."

"Is this about the eyes again? He's right, man. You've been talking about this since the beginning of this summer. Why not just go to the house?" Vince chimed in.

"That's easier said than done. When was

the last time you explored a house where a pair of floating eyes lived?" asked Stephen.

"I can't exactly remember a time when floating eyes followed me," Mark shot back.

"Just do it. What do you have to lose?"

Stephen considered Vince's question. He *didn't* have anything to lose. And he wanted desperately to figure out who watched him and why. Exploring the McCallister house might've not been as dumb a suggestion as it sounded.

"Are you stupid or something? What are you doing?" Matt said as he stared at Stephen, who struggled to turn the doorknob. Stephen turned toward Matt.

"Your mouth is like a motor. Does it ever stop running?" Stephen asked.

"Dad is never going to let you leave this house," said Matt with a grin on his face.

"What makes you so sure?"

"Well, for one," Matt said as he started to walk toward Stephen, "it's pretty obvious that you're up to no good." Matt lifted the flashlight from Stephen's arms and flashed it briefly in his face. "What's all this stuff for anyway?"

"I'm headed out. And what stuff?" Stephen asked, pretending not to know what Matt was talking about. It was none of Matt's business, even if he was older.

Matt chuckled. "Hmm, well let's see here. You've got a flashlight, which I don't think you'd be needing if you were staying inside tonight. Here's a can of bug spray. Another indicator that you probably won't be staying in to bake muffins tonight. And last, but certainly not least, you're dressed like you're going to rob a bank. C'mon... What's going on?" Matt asked, smiling.

"I told you," Stephen said. "I'm going out. I don't owe you an explanation anyway. Mom didn't put you in charge before she left. Besides, you come and go when you want to. I don't say anything when you leave."

"You're only eleven. I'm fifteen. Know what that means? Only three years until adulthood. Dad trusts me more because I'm older. Now fess up. Where are you going?"

"Yeah, alright. Give me my flashlight back," Stephen said as he grabbed his black hoody from the coatrack and reached his hand out for the flashlight.

"Oooh, a black hoody too? Black sweatpants, black T-shirt, black hoody. There's no way anyone's ever going to suspect anything," Matt teased as he shined the flashlight under his own pudgy face.

Carrying a flashlight and bug spray might've seemed weird for someone who didn't play *Dead Zombie Attack Part V*, but Stephen knew better than to be without it. What else was he going to use to spray in case of an attack? How else would he see in the dark house? "Give that back! I'm going to—"

Stephen could hear his father's footsteps. He crammed the flashlight and bug spray underneath the stairwell.

"Hey, sport. Going somewhere?" His father asked as Stephen walked away from the stairwell.

Matt had a devilish grin on his face as he watched Stephen hesitate.

"I think I heard a couple of guys say they were going to the arcade," Stephen said. "I'm going to go...just...hang out..."

"Your mother's flight gets in tonight. I'm sure she'd want to see you when she arrives. What's the special occasion?"

"No...no occasion. Just going to hang out," Stephen said defensively.

"I'm glad to see you trying," Stephen's father said. "But you're back in this house by 9:00 p.m. and no later. It's already starting to get dark. Plus, I've got to pick your mother up from the airport. When I get back, I expect to see you in bed."

"Yeah, I will be. Thanks," Stephen said nervously, trying to search for the doorknob. If he wanted any part of exploring the McCallister house today, he knew he'd better hurry. He'd have to leave his bug spray and flashlight behind.

"Stephen?" his father shouted after him as he left.

"Yeah?" Stephen asked, poking only his small head through the door.

"Next time, ask," he said assertively.

"Huh?"

"Next time you want to go out, ask. This isn't like Hinsdale. We're new and don't know very many people. I'd like to keep a close eye on you for now. Too many dangers in the world today."

"Okay, Dad," Stephen said. He had no time to wallow in his usual "don't you trust me" and "this isn't fair" thoughts. Today he had a much larger mission.

He slammed the door behind him and headed toward the McCallister house.

CHAPTER 4

The rain from earlier made the wind feel colder than usual. Wendy rubbed her forearms, shivering as the breeze blew her ponytail in back of her.

Cool nights in June were unusual in Wally Heights. Wendy wished she'd been thinking clearly when she left the house. Her mind felt crowded, as if all of her thoughts were spilling over. But no. She couldn't go back. Nothing was worse than facing Grandpa Lou when he was mad. Not even rain and bitter cold.

Wendy walked against the strong wind as her clothes blew against her. The cold helped clear her thoughts. She had no idea where she might end up or when she might turn around and head home, but something guided her: a strange magnetism that she couldn't explain and didn't mind.

She looked carefully at all of the random Wally Heights houses she passed. They all looked so different in the night. On snowy, winter school days, they looked so perfect—

like rows of white, square blocks. On summer days, they looked vibrant with little beams of light reflecting from the windows. But on cold summer nights like this one, Wally Heights and its houses appeared ordinary. Shingles fell off of some of the roofs and dead green and brown weeds crowded the gardens of some of the older residents. Wally Heights had been the only place in all of Alabama that got snow. It had proved to be a wonderful tourist attraction in colder months. "White Paradise" was what the old mayor used to call it. Wendy longed for the comfort and familiarity of "White Paradise." Instead, she saw a much scarier sight as she stared at the building that was now in front of her.

It was the McCallister house. It sat next to an empty parking lot that was riddled with potholes and litter. Every door and window had been broken into and red crumbled brick surrounded it. A long, rectangular loose board sat propped against the doorway, blocking all views of what lay inside.

The same fear that Wendy had been trying to contain since this afternoon crept up on her again. Her insides felt like an inflating balloon. How had she gotten here? She certainly hadn't intended to go to the McCallister house. It had been the place that scared her most. She wanted to turn and sprint, flailing her arms and screaming for help, but she couldn't draw attention to herself. If anyone saw her acting in such an unruly way, they would take her back to Grandpa Lou whether she liked it or not.

Wendy stood in front of the house, frozen, watching to see what she could see. She felt drawn to it, like there was something that she needed to know.

The wind blew small crumbles of red brick into Wendy's eyes. She rubbed them furiously, trying to get the sting out of them. And then she heard it. Another young person's voice. It was faint and coming from just beyond the doorway of the McCallister house. Wendy remained calm. *Probably just the wind,* she tried to convince herself. And she might have wholeheartedly believed that if she didn't hear it again in the very next instant. She squinted her eyes and looked toward the house again. Though she couldn't make out what they were saying, she was sure that she had heard someone inside.

"Hello?" she asked softly as she cautiously walked toward the house.

No answer.

"Hello?" she asked a little louder as she walked closer. She stopped. There was another sound coming from outside of the house. A thud. It seemed like the sound of someone dropping something. Wendy ran and hid, sliding in a small, triangular space just underneath the McCallister house's old, wooden stairwell. She peeked out and saw the new boy from next door picking up something from the ground. He was still quite a ways away. Wendy hoped he wouldn't see her. But where could she go from here? She knew for certain that the new boy would see her if she tried to leave.

Would the new boy tell Grandpa Lou that he saw her at the McCallister house? She wondered if he would think she was weird if she was at some old, abandoned house. Wendy ducked underneath the stairwell again until she could hear the new boy's footsteps. The smell of mold and wet leaves clogged her nostrils. She held her breath and waited for the new boy's footsteps to pass her. When she could finally hear him come closer, Wendy brushed the leaves off of her pants, preparing to come out of the bottom of the stairwell.

But instead she heard the footsteps tiptoeing on top of the creaking stairs. *What reason does the new boy have to visit the McCallister house?* Wendy thought. Could he have seen the eyes at the town meeting earlier, too? Wendy quietly sank back into a pile of leaves underneath the stairwell. She wrapped her arms around her knees carefully so that the new boy couldn't hear her.

CHAPTER 5

Stephen knew what he had to do and there wasn't much time to do it—his 9:00 p.m. curfew was quickly approaching. He remembered Vince and Mark's advice from earlier; they were right. If Stephen was ever going to find out who or what watched him from the McCallister house and what followed him in the meeting that day, he had to act fast.

A thin sheet of fog fell over the treetops. Stephen dug his fingertips into his palms. As he stood at the bottom of the McCallister house steps and stared at the doorway, he was sure that he could make out the faint outline of a pair of eyes in the window, glaring through the darkness.

Stephen froze as he watched the eyes, his forehead growing hotter and wetter with each second. He felt a tightening in his chest, but he refused to run away like the girl at the town meeting had. He had to know what watched him.

The eyes, by now, had turned toward him and seemed to have settled upon watching him just as intently as he watched them. The wind blew debris and grass across the window. The eyes stared off to the side, looking longingly at the disheveled pile.

The cool air made Stephen's nostrils flair a little. With each step toward the doorway, his stomach turned. He had never entered a ghost's house before.

Too afraid to breathe, he listened for any sounds. Carefully, he pushed the weighty board to the side of the doorway, making a slit just small enough for his arm. He ran his hand along a dusty wall as he struggled to find the light switch. On the way to the McCallister house, he had dropped and broken the spare flashlight that he kept in the pocket of his jogging pants. *So much for being able to see in the dark.*

Stephen grunted as he pushed the board aside and made the opening bigger. The unbalanced board flopped on the ground with a thud sending dust and dirt flying upward. The small amount of sunlight that was left from the day shined inside of the house. He stepped back and looked around the barely lit room. He thought he had heard someone cough. Could ghosts cough? His palms started to sweat again. His heart pumped harder.

Stephen reluctantly stepped inside. He

was shocked by the size of the McCallister house. It was much bigger than it appeared on the outside.

There were a bunch of bricks, piles of dust, a shoe that the rats had gotten a hold of, and spider webs everywhere. He could see the shiny, thin outline of hundreds of webs, highlighting the creatures caught in them.

To his right, a long winding stairwell with scratches in the wood led to the top of the house. To his left was a small room, seemingly for storing something. It was bare and dusty and didn't look very much like some place you would take pleasure in entertaining anyone.

Straight ahead, he saw a long corridor with numerous rooms on each side. The hairs on his neck rose. He began to tremble and sweat a little. He walked toward the exit. "Just some old house," Stephen said under his breath.

But as he turned his back to leave, he heard something. Music. Guitar music. When he turned to face the corridor again, he started to grow hot and dizzy. There in the corner of the main room by the house's entrance sat a floating guitar and deep brown eyes above it. The guitar looked old. The strings were corroded and the image of a crystallized rose on the guitar's neck was faint and faded. But still, the guitar made the most harmonious sound. It was the best music Stephen had ever heard. He watched as each string plucked itself. The guitar tuner turned as more strings plucked themselves. The pair of large brown eyes stared at him blankly.

More and more pairs of eyes surfaced: blue ones, green ones, bright ones, weary ones.

Stephen backed up toward the front door, nervously watching the eyes in front of him. He was too surprised to scream and too agitated to fight. His hands shook fiercely as he planted them firmly on his thighs. He wished that his heavy, dark hoody were a light, breathable, sleeveless shirt.

"What's your name?" a child's voice rang out. Stephen stopped stepping back. He looked all around him, but saw no children. *Where did that voice come from?*

"Run along, Isabel. You'll frighten the poor boy."

"I will not. Can he hear us, father?" she asked.

"I should hope so or else we've already wasted a great deal of time. You never can be too sure of these things, though," the eyes answered. The guitar played an upbeat folk tune melody.

Stephen looked around frantically for children or a father. He could see nothing but sets of eyes. He heard the stomps of many feet as the eyes leapt every which way. He opened his mouth to speak, but it felt too dry for words. "Who's there?" he managed to belt out in a squeaky voice he didn't recognize.

"Why does the boy look so frightened?" said another booming voice. The music and footsteps stopped. All eyes stiffly turned to Stephen. For what, he didn't know, but he certainly didn't want to stay to find out. He ran as fast as he could toward the door. Everything around him was a shaking blur.

"Going somewhere?" Stephen heard a boy's voice say. Almost instantly, the long wooden board that had fallen to the ground, rose and propped itself up against the doorway. A set of beady eyes stood in front of the board.

Stephen screamed and tried to run forward, but there they were: sets of eyes crowding around him.

"Father, do you think he really can hear us? Is he the one?" an older teenage male voice asked.

Stephen's leg started to shake. "Leave me alone. Why do you keep watching me?" he finally managed to shout in his normal voice. But the eyes didn't answer. They crowded around Stephen until the air felt too stuffy to breathe, too crowded to focus. His voice planted itself in his throat and formed a thick knot.

"So you *can* hear us...simply amazing," said the brown eyes. The eyes shifted from Stephen to the front door. "John, bring the other one in too. Don't let her get away either." Stephen watched as the beady green eyes made their way to the doorway and removed the wooden board again. It landed with a gentle plop and kicked up dust. "You over there," the voice from the brown eyes said. "Please come out. If you can hear us, come out now!"

CHAPTER 6

Stephen's breaths were shallow by now. He could feel lines of sweat sliding down his back. His normally gel-spiked hair was now matted. The voice's words repeated in his mind: *Don't let her get away either.* Either? Since when didn't he have the choice to leave? *I have to get out of here,* Stephen thought. But how would he do that? The eyes surrounded him on all sides in a circle. He was helpless and pitted in the middle like a bull's-eye.

Someone else started to walk into the doorway. He watched as a tall, slender girl with loose, messy hair came walking up the steps. She looked like a news reporter with red-rimmed glasses and slightly bucked teeth. Stephen recognized her almost instantly. It was his next-door neighbor, the screaming girl at the town meeting.

He started to yell at her. To warn her that his curiosity maybe hadn't been worth it and that now he was practically being held hostage by a group of...things. But his fear overwhelmed him. He watched helplessly as the girl stood in the doorway, looking at the eyes like she was scared and hypnotized. She screamed and ran out of the house and down the steps. This time, a pair of blue eyes darted after her.

"Don't even think about it," the green eyes said to Stephen. "You scream like the girl and I am not going to be very happy. You don't want to do that: make me unhappy."

"He's got a real bad temper," the young girl eyes said. Her brown eyes seemed to get bigger when she said the word *temper.*

Seconds later, the girl who ran from the doorway was walking back into the house. Her look had gone from curiously afraid to terrified.

No. What are you doing? Stephen thought, hoping his thoughts made it to the girl. *Get out of here!* Why would anyone want to come back to this place?

As the girl walked through the doorway, the blue eyes followed. Stephen saw that a piece of glass was pressed to the girl's back. She walked stiffly toward Stephen and the eyes led her next to him in the middle of the circle. He could hear the girl's heavy breathing.

I need to get out of here, Stephen thought again. It was something that his mind had told him to do over and over, but his body couldn't bring itself to follow. He studied the piece of glass that the blue eyes had now set on the floor. He wondered if the eyes could chase him quick enough if he darted out of the house, or if anyone in Wally Heights would hear his screams.

"Simply amazing!" the brown eyes exclaimed as they looked at the girl. "You can hear me, too."

"What do you want? Why are you holding us here?" Stephen finally managed to ask.

A look of amusement came over the brown eyes. The other eyes stared at Stephen and Wendy curiously. "You're going to help us. Both of you. We want to thank you in advance," said the brown eyes.

"I'm not helping you with anything!" the girl yelled. Stephen wished that she would shut up. It was obvious that they wouldn't be helping the eyes, but the eyes didn't have to know that.

"What are your names?" a pair of wise, gray eyes asked.

"Uh, Larry," Stephen said.

The brown eyes laughed. "Larry?" The green eyes stormed from the room and toward the corridor.

"Yes," Stephen said nervously. Maybe if they didn't know his name, they'd have a harder time finding him when he ran.

"I've been on this earth for hundreds of

years. You don't think I know when I'm being lied to?" the brown eyes said.

Hundreds of years? Stephen thought. So these things *were* ghosts. They had to be.

"I've followed you long enough to know that you're not Larry," said the brown eyes.

"I—I'm sorry," Stephen started. But a loud noise interrupted him: an enraged scream. Stephen watched as a white mug flew toward the wall and shattered into pieces. The green eyes stood by the corridor staring at the mess and then at Stephen.

"Son, that's enough," the brown eyes said, turning to the green eyes. The brown eyes looked at Stephen again. "He doesn't like being lied to," the voice said. "And neither do I."

Stephen stood quietly, looking at the sets of eyes that stared at him blankly.

The gray eyes stepped forward. "Everything that we're going to tell you today is truth. None of it is a lie. We'd appreciate the same courtesy."

"Dear me. I was afraid that this might happen. I was afraid you'd lie, even on a question as simple as 'what's your name?'" said the brown eyes.

"I didn't mean it. I was scared," Stephen said quickly. "Stephen. My name is Stephen."

"Ah, I'm afraid that your honesty is just a bit too late, my good boy. See, you've shown me that you're not completely trustworthy," the brown eyes explained.

"I am. Honestly. I—you can trust me," Stephen said.

"Me too. You can trust me," the girl chimed in.

"Oh, I'm sure I can. Because I will make you trust me," the brown eyes said.

The green eyes went toward the corridor again and came back to the circle with a set of sharp, shiny, silver knives that floated a little beneath the eyes. He went around in a circle handing out the knives to the other sets of eyes. *This is it,* Stephen thought. *I've got to make a run for it now.*

Just after the green eyes handed two out of four sets of eyes their knives, Stephen darted for the door, but soon fell on his face. He felt the tip of a knife catch in his sweatpants as he dropped to the floor.

The brown eyes hovered over Stephen and looked at him as they spoke. Stephen could see the girl still standing in the middle of the circle. She stared at him in horror, but she didn't dare speak a word. "Stephen, Stephen. You continue to disappoint me. If you try to get away one more time, I'm afraid I'm going to have to hurt you for real this time."

Stephen nodded cautiously and tried to lift himself from the floor. "Stay down there," the brown eyes said. Stephen did as he was told. "You," the brown eyes said, looking at the girl. "What's your name?"

"Wendy," the girl said as though she was unsure of her own name.

"Wendy, you lie down too. Just like Stephen. Right where you are. Go on," said the brown eyes.

Wendy didn't bother to protest or speak. Instead, she lay in the middle of the circle, staring at the eyes that looked down on her.

The blue eyes and green eyes each walked to opposite sides of the room, their knives still floating just below them.

"There'll be one outside of each door, just in case you should think to run again," the brown eyes said, looking at Stephen and then Wendy.

I'm doomed, Stephen thought. *This is it and it's all my fault.* Why did he have to know so badly what watched him?

For a second, Stephen lay on the floor, not knowing what to expect. The adult brown eyes stood watch over Stephen, while the smaller, brown eyes stood next to Wendy. The wise, gray eyes had left the room a few moments earlier and Stephen had no desire to guess what the eyes would bring back with them this time. *Please, God,* Stephen thought, *if you just get me out of this one thing, I promise I'll never investigate another thing. I promise.*

No sooner had Stephen thought this, than

the gray eyes bounced back into the room with four long strands of rope.

"Who are you?" Stephen demanded, as the gray eyes coiled the scratchy rope around his wrists and ankles. The gray eyes didn't answer. Instead, they walked toward Wendy with the other two pieces of rope.

"Ronald Hideaway," the brown eyes announced proudly. "Pleasure making your acquaintance. These are my children," said Ronald. "My boys Jack and John, and my darling daughter Jennifer. My father, Percy, is who's done the wonderful job of tying you up."

Stephen looked over at Wendy, who squirmed and struggled with having her arms tied behind her back, and then over at the gray eyes that were making their way back to him.

"What do you want? Why are you doing this?" Wendy yelled.

"What do you want from us? What did I ever do to you?" Stephen asked.

"That is a long story," said Ronald as he settled next to Stephen and Wendy. "But first you must know how we came to be. Would you like to hear?"

Stephen looked in back of him and out of the doorway at the pair of beady eyes that stood watch. His eyes caught the glimmer of the knife that floated just below the eyes. The bending tree shadows on the sidewalk made the eyes look even more menacing.

Stephen stared back at Ronald, who waited with anxious and excited eyes for him to answer. Had anybody been out that night, Stephen might've taken his chances at trying to escape again. Some passerby was bound to see the floating knife and maybe even the set of eyes. And he couldn't have possibly tied himself up with rope or cut open the back of his own sweatpants. Somebody would have to know that someone did this to him.

But aside from the neighborhood watch that patrolled the streets whenever they felt like it, Wally Heights was nearly deserted at night. Stephen looked at Ronald and reluctantly nodded yes. He stared at Wendy, who seemed hesitant, but also nodded. A small jolt of fear, dread, and excitement shot through Stephen. Today was the day that Stephen would put to rest the mystery of the eyes that followed him.

CHAPTER 7

Ronald wasted no time telling his story. Stephen could see Ronald's eyes bounce toward his side of the room, as though he were walking to him. He was grateful that the eyes didn't go into the long hallway instead. Ronald must've forgotten that he was holding a knife because, as he talked, it flailed every which way and sparkled even when no light hit it.

"We are the Hideaways. My, I've been waiting for years to explain this! And now, someone can finally hear it," said Ronald excitedly, his eyes focusing on Stephen and Wendy. Stephen's eyes met Wendy's before he stared at Ronald again.

"Long ago," Ronald started, "we were a highly esteemed family. Most everyone in our town was, really. We were not a very rich people, but we weren't poor either. Everyone was an equal in nearly every respect. But I'm afraid that no matter how just this world is, there are people in it who seek to make it unjust."

"Papa, what's unjust?" a lower set of eyes asked.

"Quiet for now, dear. We've got visitors," Ronald said calmly. The low, brown eyes bashfully stared at the ground.

Stephen began to see fog— and no ordinary fog, either. The fog was so opaque that it covered sections of the house.

It gathered from every corner of the room and filled the air until one large, thick opaque cloud formed. Inside of the cloud, Stephen saw men, women, and children clad in lengthy gowns, tunics, and hats with yellow feathers in them. The men and children laughed and danced with delight while the smitten women extended their hands for dances. Everyone was gathered in what looked like a hall with several large pillars at every corner. And the gold! It was everywhere. Stephen saw gold cups, gold plates, golden shields, golden locks on women and children. He couldn't take his eyes off of the fog. Inside the cloud seemed to be another world and Stephen desperately wanted to immerse himself in it—anything to get himself out of the nightmare that he was in.

"He always was a good storyteller," Stephen heard the other adult say.

Who are those people in the cloud? Why are

they dressed that way? Stephen thought. He sat and stared curiously at the fog, his wrists squirming behind his back from the tight rope.

"Don't be alarmed. All you have to do is watch the cloud. Watch what happens inside," Ronald said.

"What am I looking at? What is this?" Stephen asked Ronald, finally turning away from the fog. He glanced over at Wendy, who stared at it like she hadn't ever seen fog before.

"The story of how we came to be. This is what you must know before you know why we've been watching you."

CHAPTER 8

Stephen remained silent as the images in the cloud of smoke became vivid. He became more enthralled as the colors strengthened and the people's movements became steady and fluid. Ronald's words began to meld into one long sound until Stephen could no longer recognize them. The fog encircled the entire room and suddenly, Stephen felt as though he was a part of Ronald Hideaway's distant memory.

"Papa tells reeeeal good stories," Stephen heard the young girl say.

Inside of the fog, music boomed from every end of the large room. It was strange music that Stephen hadn't heard before. It was upbeat and sweet with the dissonance of harps and the short chords of fiddles.

Several long tables, decorated with slender, lit candles and plate covers that looked like the tops of bells, sat to the side of a polished ballroom floor. Two chandeliers hung from separate ends of the room.

What was most striking was what everyone wore. Every woman wore a dress that hugged the top of her tightly and made her bust push up a little. The bottom of the dresses flared out in an upside-down U-shape, like there was an umbrella underneath. Each dress swayed and changed direction with the tempo of the music.

The men wore puffy-sleeved shirts with tight pants and boots. No man's hair was shorter than his shoulders and, unlike the women's tight updo, the men's hair swung rhythmically as they graciously danced with the women.

But then, as the people were dancing, a set of gold-carved double doors swung open, knocking a lit candle onto one of the tablecloths. The music stopped. The expressions of glee on the faces of the women and children turned sour. The men stood in front of their wives, shielding them with one hand and one foot planted forward.

A short, but rather large, balding man grinned a yellow-toothed smile as he surveyed the room. He moved his finger along his thick, long eyebrow and then along his crooked teeth. Some fire from the fallen candle had gotten on the man's tunic, but he didn't seem to mind. Instead he used the palm of his hand to calmly pat out the fire as he walked toward the frightened crowd.

Stephen heard Ronald's faint whisper outside of the fog: "That's Sir Edward Duke."

"Did someone," the intruder started, "have a party and forget to invite his dearest wishmaster?" he asked with a half grin on his face.

"How did you find out about this?" a tall, sturdy man asked as he stepped out of the crowd.

The intruder chuckled. "You know as well as I that where there is a gathering of people, there are wishes to be made. I've been around for some of the century's most prolific discoveries. The very land that you stand on, in fact." The intruder stepped toward the man and lowered his voice to an antagonizing whisper: "Did you really think that I couldn't find out about a mere party?"

Speechless, the man stepped back into the crowd.

Some women started to cry while others tried to appear brave, leaving themselves in the open to confront the man. *What's so scary about this man? And what's a wishmaster?* Stephen thought.

Sir Edward Duke spotted a man who trembled so tremendously that the clothes he wore fell from one shoulder. He turned to the man and bellowed, "One wish and one wish only!"

"Please, sir...spare me. I wish for nothing."

"You can be prided with all the world's riches and still you want nothing?" The man sank into deep thought. A longing in his eyes came forth. Cries rang from every inch of the room:

"Don't do it!"

"Have some mercy!"

"Mortimer, I urge you to reconsider!"

But Mortimer had already been overcome by an overwhelming sense of greed. "I wish for one million shillings," Mortimer said softly, but confidently. Gasps could be heard all around the court.

"It is done," Sir Edward Duke yelled.

A bag of one million shillings appeared next to Mortimer. He grabbed the large sack and tugged it to him.

"Anything else, my good man? Anything at all? The world is yours. Will you only stop at one million shillings?"

Mortimer humbly looked down at the floor, still gripping his bag of shillings. "I thought you were only granting one wish," Mortimer said.

"One wish and another for good measure!" Sir Edward Duke shouted. "Alas, will you do nothing for your kingdom? The very people who have stood by your side and braved the attacks of the Water Creek people?" Sir Edward Duke shouted. The ladies grabbed onto their children protectively. Some fathers stood squarely in the corner, yet dared not lunge forward.

A man with long, wavy golden hair and a sturdy physique remained crouched underneath one of the tables.

"That's me," Stephen heard Ronald's voice say in the distance. Stephen continued to watch the fog closely, trying to ignore Ronald's voice.

Mortimer confidently and very slowly rose to his feet.

"Well?" Sir Edward Duke asked, as his eyes followed Mortimer. "Another wish to even things up a little?"

Again everyone pleaded with Mortimer.

"No, don't do it!"

"We don't need anything else!"

"He'll trick you!"

"We are a happy people! Nothing else!" the people shouted at Mortimer.

"How do I know you're not tricking me?" Mortimer asked Sir Edward Duke hesitantly. "I mean...how do I know this isn't all a setup?"

"Check your bag. Are the shillings in it not real?" Sir Edward Duke asked Mortimer.

Mortimer opened the large brown sack of shillings, and stared cautiously at Sir Edward Duke.

"Well? Go ahead and check. I mean you no harm, my good man. I am only here to grant wishes," said Sir Edward Duke.

Mortimer picked out one of the golden coins. He looked at the markings on it closely and then dropped it to the floor with a clank. He picked the coin up and turned to the crowd, who watched anxiously. "It's real," he said with greed in his eyes. "One million shillings...one million...it's real!" he yelled. "It's really real!"

Sir Edward Duke smiled coyly, satisfied that he had gained Mortimer's trust. "Of course it is. Is that not what you asked for? You can rest assured that whatever else you ask for, I'll give. Anything. Name it, my good man."

Mortimer stared back at the crowd and then at Sir Edward Duke. Mortimer planted one hand underneath his chin, thinking.

"Well?" asked Sir Edward Duke.

"I wish," Mortimer started, his gaze shifting from the floor to Sir Edward Duke. "Well... if I may..." Mortimer cleared his throat. "The people of Water Creek have been ever so cruel...but if only they knew and believed we meant them no harm, their attacks would cease."

Everyone grew silent as a solemn acceptance made its way around the room. There were no more protests, no more cries, and no more moans. Short shallow breaths permeated the air.

Everyone silently looked at Mortimer as he

stood in the face of Sir Edward Duke. Mortimer parted his thin lips to speak. "I wish, oh that I wish, that the people of Water Creek could see through our people, the people of Teafall, so that our kind motives and good hearts could be made obvious to them. If only they could look us in our eyes and see the good in us. "

Sir Edward Duke smirked as he looked at the frightened crowd. And then came his bellowing—"It is so!"

The women continued to hold their children flat against their bosoms, and when Sir Edward Duke left, everyone stayed crouched. Milliseconds upon seconds upon minutes had gone by and when everyone figured him to be gone for good, they rose.

Outcries of shame and disdain were turned into congratulations and praise for Mortimer. He became the town's hero for the moment. Everyone had long wished for peace for Teafall and finally, they would receive it.

The room exploded into song and dance. The gentleman with the golden locks scooted his strong body from underneath the small, wooden table.

Everyone danced to slow songs and fast songs and merry songs and ceremonial songs until a shrill cry rang loudly throughout the room. Stephen had never heard such a horrific scream—not even in *Dead Zombie Attack Part V*.

It was the cry of a lady. Everyone backed away until she was left alone, in the middle of the hall, screaming the shrillest of screams. She wrapped her lithe fingers around a drinking glass and screamed again, nearly dropping the glass on its bottom. People watched as she turned the glass upside down and stared into the bottom. "Have you gone mad?" a few people cried out.

"My reflection! It's gone. Look for yourself if you think I've gone mad." And so everyone did. Sure enough, she did not have a reflection. And neither did anyone else.

"He won't get away with this," a knight said furiously as he stormed toward the double doors, sword and shield in hand.

"Wait!" another one of the knights yelled. "You can't face him alone. I'm coming with you."

"I'm coming along too. We have a better chance of confronting him in strong numbers," said another knight.

Furious, the group of knights rode on horseback to find Sir Edward Duke. Mortimer was nowhere to be seen.

Stephen could very clearly see the muscular horses galloping through the forest terrain, but their riders were a mystery. Their reins wiggled in the air as though someone was holding them, but Stephen could no longer see the knights' hands or bodies. Now he saw them as outsiders did: multiple sets of angry, determined eyes.

As a split in the path came about, half of the horses went left and the other, right. Stephen could feel one of the horses rapidly wind around a path. He grew lightheaded as the horses finally slowed down at a riverbank.

Sir Edward Duke sat by the riverbank, peacefully throwing pebble after pebble in the water.

"What have you done?" Stephen heard a man in the fog shout.

Sir Edward Duke turned around curiously. When he saw the group of angry eyes, a smile spread over his face.

"Answer us at once!" another shouted.

"Wishmaster or not, I'll show *him* how to disappear!" another man yelled.

"Have you the audacity to be angry?" Sir Edward Duke antagonized. "I gave what Mortimer asked for, did I not?"

None of the eyes answered. Instead they inched toward Sir Edward Duke.

"What are you going to do? Hit me?" Sir Edward Duke laughed. "Go ahead. I'd like to see it."

Suddenly, the fog and the people in it condensed, and in three seconds, it was as though there had been no fog at all. All of a sudden, one thing made sense to Stephen: Sir Edward Duke had dared the angry knights/

eyes to hit him. That must've meant that the Hideaways couldn't touch anyone. But the slash on the back of his pants leg was real. They might not have been able to directly touch him, but they could hurt him, Stephen concluded.

"It didn't end there, did it?" Wendy asked. Stephen stared at her, surprised that she had chosen then to speak, but she had been right. It couldn't just end there. Nothing made sense yet.

"No...it didn't. There were some things that we didn't find out until much later," Ronald said.

"What did I just watch and what do you want from me?" Stephen asked Ronald, realizing again where he was.

"You watched Sir Edward Duke inflict his cruelest joke on us yet. He was the town's wishmaster. In those days, every town had one. They'd allow you to make a wish, but rarely would it be a wish beneficial for the wisher."

Stephen stared at Ronald, confused.

"Sir Edward Duke was the fellow who barged into the party...the one with one eyebrow?" Ronald said, trying to make Stephen understand. "Anyway," Ronald continued, "It's said that wishmasters were put in towns to prevent greed. No one knows the exact reasoning, really. The day they disappeared was indeed a happy one. I suppose greediness grew too great to prevent, and there became no more need for them," Ronald explained.

"I'm sorry that he did that to you. I really am, but I swear I don't have anything to do with it," Stephen said. "Could you please let me go? I need to get home."

"Me too," Wendy said.

"In good time, yes, you can go home," Ronald said. "There's still more that you need to know."

"What do you want?" Stephen asked.

"I would like for you to stop asking that question long enough to listen. Can you do that, Stephen?" Ronald said.

Stephen didn't answer. Any reply would probably set the eyes off at any moment, and Ronald, Percy, and little Jennifer still held their knives like they were ready to use them at a moment's notice.

Ronald continued. "What Mortimer wished for was granted in one way or another. He wished that the people of Water Creek could look into our eyes and see straight through us. Well, my good boy and gal, he got his wish. We are all see-through and our eyes, I'm sure, you can see very well. Or so we've been told. To each other we look just as real and whole-bodied as Wendy looks to you," Ronald said, staring at Stephen.

Stephen stared at the sets of eyes, not knowing what to say or think.

"Please let me go," Wendy pleaded.

Ronald paused and looked at both of the children before he spoke. "Not so fast. Wendy, you have a basement. Is that true?"

Wendy hesitated before eventually saying, "Yes."

"Ah, I thought so. There's a reason that you can see us. Only those children that can help us can see us. And, well, now that we know you're the ones in Wally Heights with a basement *and* you're capable of seeing us, we know that we have the right ones. You're going to help us," said Ronald.

"Help you how?" Stephen said. "I think you probably meant to capture somebody else. I don't have a basement."

"But you can see me, and that is proof enough that you are meant to help us too," said Ronald.

Stephen shook his head no. There was no rule saying he *had* to help—nothing to make him feel like he was obligated.

"You can make us human again. And the key to it all is in that basement of yours," Ronald said as he stared at Wendy, who still lay on the floor. "Do you know how lonely this is? To be practically invisible to others?"

"I'm not in this, and I can't help you," Wendy said.

"Oh, but you are. Wishmasters only live in basements and you, my lady, have a basement. You and Stephen are to help us. Make a wish to Sir Edward Duke and make us human again," said Ronald.

"Please just leave me alone. You have the wrong kid. I don't know anything about lifting a curse," Wendy said as her voice cracked.

"No. I have exactly the right children. It's your basement, so you must lift the curse. Stephen, you are her neighbor. You must help her."

"I don't think I can. I—"

"I'm afraid I'm not being clear enough. We are not *asking* for your help. You will help," said Ronald as he moved closer to Stephen.

But then Stephen realized something. "You can't kill us. You need us," he said.

"Yes. But I don't need either of your families, and I don't necessarily need you two to be whole in order to complete your mission. You will do this. I have confidence in you," Ronald said.

The gray eyes walked behind Stephen and loosened the rope on his wrists and ankles. Next, he loosened Wendy's. The red marks on Stephen's hands served as a reminder that the Hideaways were at least capable of *something*; he wasn't sure that he wanted to take the chance to find out what that something was. Matt was annoying, and Mom and Dad were strict, but they didn't deserve to die or be tortured by the Hideaways.

"So, you'll do it soon. Within the next day or two. If not, I'll be seeing you, Wendy, and the rest of the family soon." Ronald let the knife drop to the floor. The metal part of it clanged against the wood. "You're free to go."

Stephen stood, trying to gain circulation in his hands and feet again. Wendy had already managed to hop up and was making her way to the doorway.

"Goodnight, Stephen. Goodnight, Wendy," the little girl eyes said, as Stephen and Wendy rushed to the door.

Stephen looked back at the little girl and then at Ronald. The look in his eyes told Stephen that if he refused to help the Hideaways, nothing in the next few days would turn out well for him.

CHAPTER 9

That night, Wendy thumped on her bed and pushed her glasses further up on her nose. She took a puff of her asthma pump, breathing in and out. Wendy couldn't get her mind off of what she had heard and seen. Her mind raced with what-ifs and stories of ghosts, and ghouls, and eyes. Her wrists ached as if the rope were still tied tightly around them.

Wendy couldn't stop thinking of Ronald's words and the way that he looked at Stephen before it was time to go. They had both run home, breathless and silent. Stephen's parents had caught him coming in late, but lucky for her, Grandpa Lou had been asleep when she came home and ran straight up the stairs.

She couldn't imagine anything happening to Grandpa Lou. He had been the only family that she knew. But did that mean involving herself in solving a centuries-old curse? How did she know that Ronald hadn't been trying to trick her?

The thought of it all made her light-headed. She started downstairs, unsure of whether or not she wanted to tell Grandpa Lou about what happened. But what would Grandpa Lou do? Call the police? Go talk to the Hideaways? There was no talking to these things, and if she was to ever save Grandpa Lou, herself, and Stephen's family, she knew she would have to lift the curse.

As Wendy made her way down the stairs, the cold sweat dried to her forehead, she heard a disappointing sound: snoring. Grandpa Lou was still asleep. Part of her hoped that he had missed her while she was gone. Another larger part of her knew that he probably hadn't.

"Grandpa Lou?" she asked softly. Now was not one of the times that she wanted to be alone. Grandpa Lou rocked back and forth in his rocker gently and snored. "Grandpa Lou?" Wendy asked a little louder. But still, Grandpa didn't budge.

Wendy's eyes crept to the basement door that Grandpa Lou's chair rocked toward. She wondered why he had *really* never allowed her down there. Did it really have something to do with the Hideaways? Was something down there? It couldn't hurt much to check things out. In fact, it seemed that things would only get worse if she didn't. Besides, even if there were something down there, Grandpa Lou would still be upstairs.

Wendy looked at the large windows and then at the space in between the ill-fitting curtains that showed the blue of midnight. She pictured sets of eyes staring intrusively at her, knocking each other out the way to get a better look at her. She wondered how long they would watch her and if they were watching her now.

Still catching her breath, Wendy walked in front of Grandpa Lou to the basement door. Maybe the Hideaways were just telling her a silly story. Maybe they had the wrong girl. Her curiosity peaked.

Wendy looked from Grandpa Lou's rocking chair to the basement door. Grandpa Lou rocked rhythmically as his head tilted toward the side of the chair. Each time the chair jolted him forward, Wendy felt her stomach drop like she was on a rollercoaster. She placed her hand on the golden knob, shivering a little from the coldness of it.

She eased the door open as she stared at Grandpa. She had expected the door to make an eerie, creaking noise, but instead, it had cracked open with no sound. Nothing stood between Wendy and the dark basement.

She pulled a small metal chain above her. A dim lightbulb lit the path of the first three basement steps. Wendy pulled the door toward her, afraid that Grandpa Lou would awaken. Her insides fluttered, her stomach ached, and for a second, she had figured that Grandpa Lou might have been right. Maybe she shouldn't have been down there. Maybe Grandpa Lou's "the stairs are bad" reason was good enough and it had nothing to do with some silly Hideaway curse.

She turned back to the door, preparing to leave. Before she pushed the door any further than an inch, the lightbulb above her flickered on and off once. Then twice. Then three times. On the third flicker, the bulb lit ceremoniously and shed light to the entire basement. Wendy stared around anxiously. She had never been in the basement, but there didn't seem to be much to fear. There were no windows for eyes to watch her and no stuffed animals to mimic the eyes' stares.

A large, red lawnmower sat in the middle of the floor among brown cardboard boxes. Colorful toys sat scattered around the boxes. In a dark corner, Wendy could see the red scooter with the loud, golden bell that Grandpa Lou told her was stolen years ago.

Wendy walked down the basement steps carefully, testing each one with her toe before she stepped on it. The sour smell of molded cardboard crawled up her nose. The dead silence made each creak of the stairs sound loud. She stepped onto the basement floor, looking back once just to make sure she wasn't being followed. For once, she didn't feel like she was being watched. The familiarity of Wendy's shiny red scooter drew her to it. She walked over to it and rang the bell twice.

And then she heard it.

It sounded like a scratching sound. Almost like someone was trying to get into the basement. *Grandpa Lou must've woken up!* Wendy thought in a panic. She ran right and then left, until she settled on hiding behind a large box that sat in a corner of the room. She tucked her arms around her knees and put one hand over her mouth to keep from inhaling the rotten smell of the box. Her arms shook as she grabbed her knees tighter.

She peeked out past one side of the box toward the top of the basement stairs, expecting to see Grandpa Lou shuffling down them, calling out her name in the crabby way that he always did. But nothing happened. The scratching had stopped too. Still too afraid to come out from her hiding place, Wendy stared at the stairs and leaned against a pile of books.

She leaned back a little more, sending a few of the heavier textbooks falling to the floor with a plop. Wendy froze and then hit herself for being so clumsy. She looked toward the stairs again, hoping no one could hear her deep breaths. But still, no one had come down the stairs.

She carefully turned around and stared up just beyond the top of the stack of books. There sat a thin wooden crack in the cemented wall: a dark blue door. Wendy leaned her ear a little closer to the door behind the tall pile of books. She thought that she heard something faint— a voice or a clawing or something else. She crawled around the books and closer to the wooden door.

She could hear a light scratching noise from just behind the door. Wendy ached to be upstairs in her room again. She ran from behind the box and to the stairwell. She wanted to dart up the stairs and forget that the house even had a basement. Her knees knocked together so hard that she thought they might collapse at any moment. Part of her wanted to forget that she lived in the house at all.

Now, everything looked as though it was reaching out to her, calling her. The motor of the red lawn mower looked as though it might start to whir; the red scooter looked as though it had been positioned differently from when she had played with it seconds earlier. And the light seemed to shine eerily on the middle of the basement floor and stairwell as though Wendy were a part of some creepy game show.

Wendy couldn't stand it any longer. She

sprinted up the basement steps, skipping two and three stairs at a time. She was glad that she hadn't shut the basement door all the way. Sweating and panicked, she pushed both hands against the door. But once she escaped, not even the familiar sight of a sleeping Grandpa Lou was enough to comfort her. She closed the door behind her, taking care not to wake him, and sprinted to her room.

She shut her bedroom door as softly as she had shut the basement door and leapt into her bed. She picked up her favorite pajamas—a pair of oversized black, bleach-stained sweatpants and a tie-dye T-shirt— and slipped them on. Her mind summoned millions of visions and sounds of ghosts. Moaning ones. Staring ones. Talking ones. Scratching ones. Threatening ones. She started to hope that she hadn't been followed up the stairs.

She reluctantly slipped her feet underneath her butterfly-print covers, clapping her hands twice to cut the light out. Unlike other children she knew, Wendy had never been afraid of the dark. It wasn't the dark that frightened her. The things that were in the dark were what scared her. And those things that scared her, she didn't wish to see.

Nervous, she shut her eyelids tightly and began to dream of cotton candy and circus elephants and Christmas trees...and eyes. She turned over on her left side and opened her eyes as cool air hit her back. Her fingertips felt cold as she moved a strand of hair out of her mouth. She felt her breaths getting shorter. She shut her eyes tightly again, this time purposely envisioning the warmth of summer, sunflowers, and hot chocolate.

A slight thud awoke her. She glanced toward her bedroom door, watching the hallway light that shined beneath it. No shadows nearby. The thud must not have been Grandpa Lou. Reluctantly, she rolled over, only to be gripped by terror.

A pair of blue eyes was at the side of her bed staring at her. Just below the eyes was her favorite stuffed bear with a single beaded, black eye missing.

CHAPTER 10

"Hey, man, I can barely hear you. Why are you whispering?" Mark asked through his gaming headset.

"Because they'll hear me," Stephen whispered. He studied his onscreen character, moving it swiftly through the level.

"Who?" asked Mark.

"My parents. I got in a little late last night," Stephen said. He shuddered when he remembered Ronald Hideaway's threat. He just couldn't seem to get rid of the image of the eyes standing over him, sharp blades pointing at him.

"Whoa, that bad, huh? Did they ground you?"

"So the eyes aren't ghosts?" Mark asked, picking up their last conversation.

"No. I mean, yes, they did ground me, but, no, the eyes aren't ghosts," Stephen confirmed. "They're people. It's complicated."

"I think you're overreacting," Stephen heard his father yell.

"Gotta go. They're arguing," Stephen whispered. He slipped off his gaming headset and shoved his game controller underneath his bedsheet. He cut the TV off and pressed his ear to the wall. If he listened hard enough, he could hear his parents in the next room arguing.

"Overreacting? Our son gets home an hour late from an already ridiculously late curfew for a ten-year-old and you think I'm overreacting? Not to mention, he comes home with marks on his hands and wrists. He hasn't said anything to us since he came in. But *I'm* overreacting? You're his father, not his friend. You're supposed to protect him," Stephen's mother shot back.

"Eleven," Stephen's father said calmly.

"What?"

"He's eleven years old, dear."

"Unbelievable! Did you just say that to me?"

A jolt of fear ran through Stephen. He had never quite heard his parents get *this* loud with each other. But none of this was his fault. He hadn't *wanted* to stay at the McCallister house, but he had to—just like he knew he didn't *want* to help break the Hideaway curse, but he had to. He couldn't imagine his family getting hurt because of him.

He pressed his ear harder against the wall until it turned bright red. His parents must have sensed that he was listening on the other end because, in the very next second, their voices lowered to a yell-whisper. Stephen could hardly hear the rest, but he hoped that staying in the house for a week straight with no video games was punishment enough. Anything more would be torture.

"The move has nothing to do with it. He will adjust," he heard his father say as he raised his voice.

"Oh, you'd give anything to stick up for that reverend, that mayor, whatever he is, wouldn't you?" said his mom.

There was more yelling and mumbling that Stephen couldn't make out.

"Fine. I'm not going to fight this one. If you think that's best, then that's what we'll do," his father said.

"Stephen!" his mother called in an angry voice.

Stephen ran as fast and quietly as he could to his bed and pretended to read a book. His hands shook as he held the book up to his face. His stomach sank as he heard his parents' bedroom door open.

"Stephen," his mother said as she appeared in his doorway next to his father. Her voice sounded soft as though she hadn't been arguing minutes before.

"Yes, Mom?"

"What happened last night?" she asked with concern in her voice.

"Nothing." Stephen hadn't bothered to tell his parents anything about what happened. If no one would believe him about the eyes watching him, no one would dare believe that they had threatened him. Besides, the Hideaways might not like it so much if he told. He decided to keep last night to himself. He would have to reverse the curse and make them go away himself.

"You don't look okay and you didn't look okay last night," Stephen's father said. "Where did you go?"

"I told you. A couple of us decided to play football after we went to the arcade. That's all," Stephen explained.

Stephen's mother and father looked at each other with concern. "We think that maybe the people that you've been hanging around...ahem, or talking to, haven't been the best influence on you," his mother said.

"Who? The guys from yesterday? No problem. I won't ever see them again."

"No...I don't think people you just met had that much influence on you," said his father.

"Who, then? Mark? Vince?" Stephen asked.

Stephen's parents stared at each other again and back at Stephen.

"What's wrong with my friends?"

"We feel that they may not be the best influence on you. Maybe it'd be best if you found someone to actually hang around with here," his mother insisted.

"So you don't believe that I was with the guys at the arcade?" Stephen asked. "I swear, Mark and Vince had nothing to do with last night!"

"This is not a debate," his mother insisted. "We're having the next-door neighbor over for dinner. She's a nice girl. There's someone to hang out with."

"What? Wendy? A girl? That's not fair! Dad?" Wendy had been all right to be with in the McCallister house, but Stephen hadn't wanted to be her friend or anything.

"Wonderful, so you already know her," said Stephen's father.

"C'mon, Dad," Stephen pleaded.

"Your father and I agreed on this already," Stephen's mother cut in.

"She's right, sport," his father confirmed— though he didn't sound convincing.

Stephen sank into his bed, dead sure that this had all been a part of his punishment. After all, what could be more nerve-racking than being threatened by a set of hostile eyes *and* making friends with a girl?

CHAPTER 11

Stephen wondered if Wendy was popular at Bean Elementary, the only elementary school in all of Wally Heights. A feeling of dread passed over him as he thought about having to start over in a new school this fall. He nervously stirred around his mashed potatoes until they looked like a mini vortex. He pictured the green eyes at the McCallister house when a small, green pea dropped in the middle of the vortex.

"Stephen, honey, don't do that. Food is not for playing," his mother said.

Matt raised his hand over his mouth to cover up a smile. He pretended to cough, letting a small chuckle slip.

"Cut it out," his father said sternly.

Everyone ate in silence. Wendy looked down at her food, taking unusually small bites. She looked strange, like a mouse nibbling at a block of cheese.

"So, Wendy, your grandfather tells us that you love science. I remember liking science when I was your age," said Stephen's mother, cutting up her steak enthusiastically.

"Yeah, I like science a lot. When I go to college, I want to major in chemistry," Wendy responded timidly.

"Wow," Stephen's mother gasped, "thinking about college at such a young age. What a wonderful influence," she chimed, looking at Stephen. Stephen pretended not to hear her and instead chose to fidget with the paper napkin on his lap.

"Great to hear! We're the newbies here, but you and your grandfather are welcome at our house anytime," Stephen's father said.

"Oh, absolutely. Stephen could use some cool friends," Matt said casually.

"Hey, I've got an idea," said Stephen's mother, before Matt could get a rise out of Stephen. "We're having a few family members over for Matt's birthday in a few days. Why don't you come and bring your grandpa? We'd love to have you."

Stephen stared at his mother angrily. It was bad enough he had to deal with his Aunt Doris's juicy red lipstick kisses. Now he would have to spend his time entertaining a guest. Stephen rolled his eyes and went back to stirring his mashed potato vortex.

"Thank you," said Wendy. "Grandpa Lou isn't feeling very well today. Wish he could have made it." Wendy looked down at her plate, continuing to eat in what Stephen thought was slow motion. It was distracting and annoying. He didn't even know of any animals that ate *that* slowly.

"You do know you can always get more, right?" Stephen said impatiently, pointing his fork toward Wendy's food.

"Stephen!" his mother yelled.

"You're actually supposed to chew your food thirty-two times before you swallow," Wendy replied.

"Fascinating," Matt commented as he stuffed his mouth full of potatoes. "You know, Stephen's species doesn't need to chew much. Everything just sort of slides on down." He lowered his voice to a whisper and leaned closer to Wendy. "Evolutionary gap."

A smile spread over Wendy's face as she tried hard to hold back a giggle.

"Matthew, cut it out," his mother yelled.

"Squirrel brain!" Stephen yelled at Matt.

"Alright, alright, cut it out," his father said.

Just then, a loud crash startled everyone. A broken glass lay on the floor in a pool of water. Stephen stared at Wendy curiously. She hadn't said anything when she dropped the drinking glass and still she remained silent. Instead she sat still and wide-mouthed as she looked toward the window. Stephen's eyes widened. It was the Hideaways. Ronald and one of his sons. Stephen could recognize those eyes anywhere. But what did Ronald want right now? Both of them appeared to be holding long, thick wooden beams. They stared intently at Wendy and then at Stephen.

Stephen's mother, father, and brother looked toward the window and back at Wendy and Stephen with confused expressions on their faces. Why hadn't his parents reacted to the floating beam? It was worse than Stephen thought. Not only were he and Wendy the only ones who could see the Hideaways, but no one else could see what the Hideaways were holding either. The Hideaways could hurt his family or him, and no one would ever know how anything happened. Stephen decided that he definitely needed to fix the curse soon.

"Is everything okay?" Stephen's father asked mainly of Wendy.

Wendy hesitated before answering. "Fine. I'm fine." She laughed nervously.

"Don't worry about it," Stephen's mom said warmly as she picked up the broken glass with a nearby dishtowel.

"It's getting a little late. We should get you home before your grandpa worries," said Stephen's father. He gently wiped the sides of his mouth with a napkin.

Wendy froze. She stared back at Stephen's father and then back at the eyes that still watched and waited outside the window.

"Hey, do you, umm, want to watch a movie?" Stephen asked Wendy. There was no telling what would happen if he opened the front door right then.

"That's a great idea. It's been a while since we've had a family movie night. I'll pop the popcorn," Stephen's father said.

Matt sighed with annoyance. Wendy nodded yes, still concentrating on the eyes that glared at her.

As Stephen's family and Wendy sat crowded around the TV, Stephen stared out of the front window. The eyes shook the wooden beams and stared at Stephen and Wendy as intensely as the rest of his family watched the movie. He understood their message clearly. The Hideaways knew where he lived and had no problem coming after him or his family. When the Hideaways seemed sure that Stephen had seen them and the thick piece of wood they carried, they hobbled off into the distance.

CHAPTER 12

It had not been fifteen minutes since Matt's birthday party started and already Stephen had failed to dodge five annoying relatives.

There was Aunt Doris, who always wore super bright red lipstick and was not shy about using it to fill Stephen's face with wet, red lip prints.

Then there was Uncle Bob who was not married to Aunt Doris, but very well could have been. They were both loud and obnoxious, but Uncle Bob always had a cigar shoved in his mouth, so when he spoke, you could barely understand what he was saying.

Aunt Doris had three sons—Floyd, Jason, and Michael—who were real jerks. All three were around Matt's age. Stephen had never bonded with his older cousins, and today was no exception. "What's up, short stack? Plan on growin' anytime soon?" one of them asked Stephen. All three of them erupted in laughter. Stephen pretended not to hear them.

Grandma Ethel, who was simply referred to by the family as "Grandma," was a sweetheart. The only problem with her was that she was a tad outspoken. The first thing that she did when she saw Matt was tap his stomach and say "*Que gordo.*" No one had ever known Grandma to speak Spanish, so Matt was not too sure about whether to respond to being called fat or to the fact that Grandma had done it in Spanish. But this was what Matt wanted. A birthday party with family that he hadn't seen in years.

Stephen sat on the couch next to one of the speakers. Old rap music played and Stephen found himself giggling at the thought of Aunt Doris and Grandma trying to dance to the music. He watched as groups of people walked about hugging each other excitedly. He wondered if Ronald was watching him right then.

"Stephen, do you want to play?" Stephen heard a small child's voice say. He looked over at his younger cousin Shawn and shook his head no.

"Not today. Maybe another time," Stephen said.

"But the party is only for today and on another day we'll be back in Philadelphia at home," the young boy said.

"Maybe later," Stephen replied. Seemingly satisfied with that answer, the little boy ran off and tapped another one of Stephen's cousins, screaming, "You're it!" The two little boys ran all around the table laughing loudly.

"Stephen, doorbell! Get the door!" Stephen heard his mom yell. He had not heard a doorbell, but it did not surprise him in the least that his mom's voice had been louder than the bell. He got up to open the door, pushing through the crowd. He rubbed the red lipstick off his cheeks one last time before he opened the door. Wendy stood in the doorway, rubbing one of her arms.

"Hey," Stephen said.

"Hey."

"You wanna come in?" he asked.

"Okay."

They walked to the couch, making sure to sit away from the speaker and everyone else. Wendy fiddled with her hands nervously, tracing the place where the rope had been just a couple of days ago. "So, how've you been?" Stephen asked Wendy.

Wendy shook her head no and looked around before she spoke. "They've been following me. I mean, they're closer now. I found one standing by my bed the same night we met Ronald. The son with the blue eyes."

"They were standing by your bed?" Stephen asked.

"Yes, and I'm sure they're following you just as closely. Yesterday, they showed up at dinner. Tomorrow, they'll probably watch you sle—"

"Stop," Stephen said, cutting Wendy off. He couldn't bear to think of them watching him while he slept comfortably underneath his covers. "We've got to do something."

For the past few days, Stephen tried knocking on Wendy's door several times, but she hadn't answered. What had Ronald meant about the door in Wendy's basement? He had to find out.

The music filled an awkward silence between them.

"Can I ask you a question?" Wendy said softly.

"Ask away," Stephen replied.

"How long have they watched you?"

"They? The Hideaways?"

Wendy nodded.

"Only for the two months that I've been in Wally Heights. How long have they watched you?" Stephen asked, half dreading the answer.

"Only for the two months that you've been in Wally Heights."

"Seriously?" Stephen asked, surprised.

"I mean, I had heard rumors about the McCallister house, saying it had been abandoned for years and that it was haunted. I had always felt something watching, but never that close. It's never been this real."

Stephen nodded, hoping she would keep talking.

"Do you think Ronald was serious about threatening our families?" asked Wendy.

"He sounded serious. What did he mean about your basement? What's in the basement?"

The color flushed from Wendy's face. "I don't know, but I hope I never find out," she answered.

"I don't think we have a choice. We have to go look. I want to see. I'll go with you," Stephen said.

"I don't know."

"What don't you know? Those things are going to get our parents if we don't get rid of Sir Edward Duke's curse." Stephen looked around him and lowered his voice to a whisper. "Don't you care? Plus the next town meeting is at the McCallister house. Who knows what they have up their sleeves?"

"Fine," Wendy said after a long bout of silence.

"What?" Stephen asked with shock in his voice. He hadn't expected Wendy to give in so easily.

"I said fine. We can look in the basement. There."

"Okay...good," Stephen said, not knowing how else to respond.

"Okay."

Although Stephen had not mentioned it in their conversation, he knew he would be knocking on Wendy's door again soon. Curing the Hideaway curse had now become the most important thing in his eleven-year-old life.

CHAPTER 13

"And so now I've got to try to help them because they're going to get rid of our families or try to hurt us," Stephen explained as he adjusted his headset.

"*Our* families?" asked Vince.

"Me and Wendy's. Haven't you been listening?"

"A girl?" Mark asked with disgust in his voice.

"It's not like that, man. They follow her too. And she's the one who needs to lift the curse, but I need to get in her basement. I've got to help because they need me too. I don't know how or why yet."

"A girl?" Vince repeated Mark's question as though Stephen hadn't said anything.

"Look, never mind. I gotta go. I told Wendy I'd come by."

"Stephen...dude...who *are* you?" Mark asked.

"Stephen!" Stephen heard his mother call from her room next door.

"Coming!" he yelled. Stephen yanked his headset off his ears. He flung it and the gaming controller underneath his messy bedsheets. He straightened out his clothes and wiped his face as though his mother would be able to tell by his appearance that he had been playing video games.

"Yeah?" Stephen asked, as he stood innocent-faced in his mother and father's bedroom doorway. His father was concentrating on his laptop screen, while his mother lay in the bed watching TV. Neither of his parents seemed to notice that the other was in the room.

"Honey, who were you talking to?" Stephen's mother asked.

"I wasn't talking," Stephen lied.

"Are you sure about that? You know you're not allowed to play your video game, right?" said his mother.

"I know... Mom?" asked Stephen.

"Yes?"

"Can I go over Wendy's house? I promise not to be there for too long and it'll only be to watch TV. I've been thinking and you're right. It's good for me to have friends. Ones in the same state," he said, staring at his father.

"You *are* on punishment," Stephen's mother said reluctantly.

"But you said that's the one person that I could hang out with," Stephen pleaded.

"You *did* say that, dear," his father said, still concentrating on his computer screen.

Stephen's mother gave his father one of those I'll-get-you type of looks. She turned to Stephen and sternly said, "You're back in here before nine. Anytime after and you will not see the light of day until you are eighteen. Is that clear?"

"Yes, it's clear. Thanks, Mom. You won't regret it," Stephen said as he breathlessly hopped down the stairs and to the door.

It had rained a ton for Matt's birthday party yesterday, so today had been one of those dreary, humid days. The mosquitos buzzed around his ears as he walked next door to Wendy's house. He looked back at his house. Something was watching him from his upstairs window.

Stephen felt lightheaded. The buzzing around his ears that had sounded minor a second ago, now sounded like thirty giant alarm clocks, all ringing simultaneously. He balled his fists tightly and squinted hard at whatever watched. But wait. There was a nose, and hair...a face. His mom. It had to be. Had he really proven himself *that* untrustworthy? If only she had known that he *had* to go to Wendy's. It was a matter of life and death. Stephen rang the bell, pretending not to see his mom looking at him. She watched him carefully as he walked inside of Wendy's house.

"So..." Wendy said hesitantly as she spoke to Stephen but stared cautiously at her grandpa. "I didn't know you were coming *today*."

"Yeah, why not?" Stephen asked curiously.

Wendy kept her eyes on her grandpa, who looked at Stephen suspiciously. For a moment, they all sat in silence while the sound of bells from a game show served as background noise.

"Soooo...this is a really nice house," Stephen said to Wendy's grandpa. "You must be really proud. It's nice and big and...big. A nice big house."

Wendy's grandpa nodded in silence, still staring at Stephen.

Stephen shifted his eyes toward the basement door and back at Wendy, who practically said "ARE YOU CRAZY?" with her eyes. Wendy's grandpa got up and walked toward the kitchen, shaking his head and mumbling something to himself along the way.

"What is the matter with you? Let's go! It's just a basement. What's the big deal?" Stephen whispered to Wendy when he was sure her grandpa was out of earshot.

"You don't understand. He won't let—" Wendy cut her sentence short and smiled at her grandfather as he gingerly walked back into the living room and grabbed a cup. As he left again to go to the kitchen, he looked at Stephen menacingly.

"OK, dude. You're really gonna have to tell your grandpa to stop staring at me like I'm some sort of monster," Stephen whispered to Wendy.

"He can be a little...cranky. He means well...I think."

"I think 'azy-cray' is the word you mean. How are we ever going to get down there?" Stephen asked as he pointed at the basement door.

"He's a heavy sleeper. We'll wait until he's asleep and go then. He's not going to let you out of his sight right now," said Wendy.

"You think?" Stephen said sarcastically.

Stephen watched Wendy's grandpa as he came back in the room and smiled, hoping he hadn't heard their conversation.

"Grandpa Lou, can I go show Stephen around Wally Heights? He's new to the neighborhood," Wendy added.

Wendy's grandpa shifted in his seat as though it pained him to acknowledge someone else speaking. "Is your homework done?" he asked.

"Grandpa, I don't have homework. We don't go back to school for another six weeks."

"Don't come back too late," he said as though he wanted Wendy to stop talking altogether.

As they walked out, Stephen followed close behind Wendy, just in case his mom was still watching. He looked back at the window of his mother's bedroom. Although he couldn't see her now, she never seemed to be too far away to have an eye on him.

"Want a tour of the neighborhood?" asked Wendy.

"Is there anything to see?" Stephen asked sarcastically.

Wendy laughed. "Barely, but it gives us something to do until Grandpa falls asleep."

They walked down Wally Heights's wet sidewalks. The grass shimmered from the rain. The trees stretched their branches generously as a handful of small birds sat on them and ate.

Still, Stephen could not let what Ronald said leave his mind. He wanted to know more about Wendy's basement. He looked off into the distance down the tree-lined sidewalks as she started to speak.

"There's Mrs. Brownsmith's house. People always say that she lives under the bridge that crosses into Spriggstown, but I don't believe that. Nobody can live under a bridge. I just think she's creepy. That's where I've seen her go when she leaves the school," Wendy said, pointing at a plain, gray house.

Maybe now isn't the right time, Stephen thought. Not when Wendy seemed so eager to be heard. But when would the right time be? Ronald Hideaway had told them that they only had a couple of days to reverse the curse. "Who is Mrs. Brownsmith?" Stephen asked, avoiding the basement talk.

"Your teacher for next year. Every sixth grader at Bean Elementary has Mrs. Brownsmith. She's the music teacher, and she takes her music seriously."

Stephen nodded in acknowledgement.

They walked toward two boys who looked to be Wendy and Stephen's age. One looked long like a stick insect and the other looked as if he could eat the stick insect boy for a meal.

Stephen nodded his head. "Hey," he said to the two boys.

The boys continued walking past Stephen and Wendy, staring ahead dryly.

"What's with them?" Stephen asked Wendy as he watched the boys walking away. He turned red with embarrassment, wishing he had never even bothered to speak.

"People sort of keep to themselves here. The real fun starts when school starts back up. That's when people hang out. After school."

"That's backwards," said Stephen.

Wendy shrugged. "I don't know. That's the way it's always been. I guess 'cause there's nothing to do here."

Wendy rounded a corner onto a block that looked exactly the same as the one they had just left. It was in the opposite direction of the McCallister house. They walked until they saw a shiny, large playground. It was perhaps the only sight in all of Wally Heights that looked like something back at home in Hinsdale. The woodchips looked dark and rich from all of the rain and despite the fertilizer smell, Stephen longed to be near it.

A group of kids inside of the playground walked about, puffing and red, laughing as they clasped their hands on top of their heads. They looked like they had just finished a *serious* game of tag.

"I thought you said people don't really hang out until school," Stephen asked Wendy, staring at the rest of the kids.

"Yeah, well, it also doesn't help that I'm not the most popular," Wendy said. She looked like she wanted to hide. Stephen thought that she might've tried to crouch behind him if she weren't at least three inches taller than him.

"Can we get next?" Stephen asked as he approached the group. He hadn't really wanted to play tag, but at least it was something to get his mind off of the Hideaways until Wendy's grandpa fell asleep for the afternoon.

"Yeah, sure...You're it," a plain-looking boy with brown hair and dingy-white gym shoes said.

Stephen nodded and waved for Wendy to follow him into the crowd of kids. Wendy tried to appear confident, slinging her shoulders back and smiling. "I'll just stay back here and watch," she said.

As soon as Stephen approached the group, they all excitedly scattered around the playground. Stephen ran as fast as he could toward the plain-looking boy who had leapt up to the top of the slide. His adrenaline made his sprint as quick as a cheetah's. *I'll get him later. Too high up for now,* Stephen thought.

He spotted another smaller boy sitting in a short tunnel nearby. He must've thought that he wouldn't get caught because he hadn't even tried to move out of the way when Stephen tiptoed toward him. The other kids yelled to warn the boy, "Ronnie! He's right next to you!" "Get out the way!" "Are you stupid? Run!" But everyone's shouts probably sounded like a confusing blur of sound to Ronnie because he just sat inside of the tunnel with his legs crossed together like a bow.

Stephen's smile grew as he approached Ronnie. His breaths quickened as he bent down to stick his hand inside of the tunnel to tag him. Ronnie must have finally gotten the clue that he was fresh tag meat because he immediately started running.

Stephen's breaths grew even quicker. His lips burned as the moisture left his mouth. He couldn't speak or even scream if he wanted to. He stared down the short tunnel in horror as he watched a pair of eyes on the other side that stared directly at him.

"You've got until tonight and then you can kiss Mom and Dad goodbye," the green eyes said.

Stephen jumped back from the tunnel and looked around at the other kids. Some had realized that Stephen had been staring through what they thought was a tunnel with no one in it and others had not noticed a thing. He looked at the tunnel again, trying not to lose track of the eyes. He had not. They were closer now. In front of him. They looked on boldly, daring Stephen to speak back to them. Stephen screamed as he squatted to the floor. His eyes watered as the pair of eyes stared down at him calmly. The other children watched him panicking on the playground floor, probably unsure of whether to run or to tell somebody that the new kid was going crazy.

And then Stephen heard something familiar that made him even more jittery. It was the same shrill scream he had heard at the town meeting. He turned around to Wendy. She was sitting on the shiny, metal seesaw, staring up. Stephen could see a pair of blue eyes on the other end of the seesaw, glaring at her.

CHAPTER 14

Stephen and Wendy ran to Wendy's front door. Stephen's legs felt unstable as if they were made of cotton.

"Do you have the key?" Stephen asked Wendy, out of breath.

"I don't know; I'm looking," Wendy said as she searched her pockets frantically. Her hands shook as she patted her pants.

"Hurry up," Stephen said impatiently as he looked behind and around him. The sprint home from the park had been a blur, and now all he wanted to do was get into Wendy's basement to see how he could make the Hideaways go away. The eyes had not hesitated to let him know that he only had until tonight to reverse the curse. They had told Wendy the same thing.

"I'm trying!" Wendy said as she looked down the street in the direction of the McCallister house.

"I'm knocking," Stephen said defiantly as he raised his hand to the door.

"Wait!" Wendy said grabbing his hand. "Grandpa won't wake up and even if he did, that would mean that we can't go into the basement. I know it's here. Just let me find it."

Stephen lowered his hand staring at Wendy as she continued to search. After a few shakes, pats, sighs, and digs, Wendy pulled out a shiny gold key and slid it quietly into the keyhole. They stepped inside, and Wendy shut the door gently behind them.

Wendy's grandpa looked to be sound asleep. His mouth was crooked to one side and he snored like a grizzly bear with a cold.

Grandpa Lou stopped snoring and started to mumble something about a war. Stephen and Wendy froze as they stared at him. Once Grandpa Lou started to snore loudly again, Wendy turned to Stephen. She seemed to be having second thoughts. "He sleeps even heavier at night. Maybe we can just wait until then," she said.

"Where's the basement?" Stephen asked, ignoring Wendy's suggestion.

Wendy pointed to the small, white door that Grandpa Lou sat in front of.

Stephen stared at the plain door. There didn't appear to be anything special about it. "We're going to have to sneak past him," Stephen strategized, still looking at the door.

"I can't do this again," Wendy said, putting

her hands to her head. "This is crazy! Do you have any idea how crazy this sounds? Curses don't exist, floating eyes can't exist, and there are no wishmasters. I can't do it."

"Again?" Stephen whispered. "You went down there without me?"

"It was just for a second and I said that I never wanted to go down there again afterwards," said Wendy.

"Well, what did you see? What was down there?" Stephen asked eagerly. He couldn't believe that Wendy hadn't told him this sooner.

"I just heard noises...I don't know."

"What type of noises? Let me see. Let's go!" Stephen whispered. "We need to do this. Look, we'll be done before he wakes up. Follow me." Stephen crept toward Grandpa Lou, watching him closely. He took large, quiet footsteps toward the basement door.

"I'm not sure about this!" Wendy yelled in a whisper.

Stephen held one finger up to his mouth to signal her to be quiet, and continued walking. His hands were filled with sweat. Something on the inside of him gripped him so tightly with fear that he was amazed his body continued to walk. When he finally made it to the basement door, Grandpa Lou started to mumble again. Stephen glanced at Wendy, who looked too afraid to even breathe.

Grandpa Lou scratched his head and leaned it farther back on the rocking chair. He snored even louder this time.

Stephen grabbed the doorknob and quietly turned it. He cracked the door a little so that the light creaking of it wasn't noticeable. He waved for Wendy to join him.

Wendy looked at Grandpa Lou fearfully and shook her head no. Stephen carefully stepped inside of the small crack in the door and waved at Wendy again. She tiptoed toward the doorway and stepped inside, her eyes on Grandpa Lou the entire time.

As Stephen shut the door behind them, Wendy reached up and pulled the metal chain connected to the basement's light. The bulb shed light to the entire basement. Stephen started down the stairs and Wendy followed.

"What are we even looking for?" Wendy asked Stephen as they stood at the foot of the basement steps.

"A book, a DVD...I don't know. Something that would help the Hideaways."

Wendy looked around and settled on staring at the small door sitting behind a pile of books. Stephen noticed her staring.

"What? What are you looking at?" he asked, watching Wendy.

"What's that?" Wendy asked, innocently.

Just behind the pile of books looked to be a crack in the wall. A door. "Is that a door?

Down here? That's weird. What's it lead to?" Stephen questioned Wendy.

"I don't know."

"Maybe that's it!" Stephen walked toward the blue door. The deep, navy paint strokes were uneven and splashed across the wood carelessly. He tried to keep his hand steady as he placed it on the knob.

"Hold on. We can't go through there. You can't open that door!" Wendy nearly yelled. She lowered her voice to a whisper. "That's where I heard the noises."

"Even better. Let's go," Stephen urged Wendy.

"Wait, how do we know that these Hideaways are telling the truth?" Wendy said in a panic.

"They've already proven that they can be dangerous. I don't want to find out whether or not they're telling the truth. We don't have a choice now. Let's go. C'mon. I'm going with you," Stephen said as he opened the door slightly.

But before he could walk in, Stephen and Wendy were pulled through the doorway like metal to magnets.

CHAPTER 15

Stephen had grown certain that he and Wendy would never land. It seemed as though they had been falling forever down a deep, wide, black space.

After what felt like minutes, Stephen and Wendy landed on a soft, velvet-like surface. Stephen stared at the floor until everything around him stopped spinning. He held his head with both hands as though it would stop his headache. He had never been so dizzy.

Once the room stopped spinning, Stephen looked around curiously. Clean, cemented bricks and grout covered the walls. Sconces with large, lit candles sat proud and erect. The room was dimly lit, but just enough for the candles to illuminate what was around them. Other than the crackle of large flames, all was disturbingly quiet. Stephen stared at a large picture of a balding, strong-looking man. Underneath, the words "All Hail Sir Edward Duke" were printed in tall, golden raised letters.

Stephen's mouth dropped a little. He tapped Wendy, who sat beside him also holding her head. "That's him!" Stephen said. "That's Sir Edward Duke."

"Impossible," Wendy whispered in awe.

"We did it! We did it!" Stephen shouted. "This must be where Sir Edward Duke lives. Now we have to find him to reverse the Hideaway curse."

"And how exactly do we do that?" Wendy asked skeptically.

Stephen shrugged. "I don't know. He's a wishmaster. Maybe we can wish the curse away. He doesn't exactly look like the type who responds to talking."

Stephen saw a flicker of something out the corner of his eye. It moved into his field of vision so fast that he jumped.

And then they came into view. Eyes. A plain pair that stared blankly at Stephen and Wendy. Had the Hideaways followed Stephen and Wendy? But why?

As the eyes moved toward the sitting children, Stephen listened for footsteps, hoping to hear their pitter patter, but he could hear nothing.

The eyes continued to glide across the tiled floor.

"Do not be afraid," said a woman's voice. "If it's Sir Edward Duke you're here to see, I can help you."

CHAPTER 16

Wendy screamed as though the eyes had threatened her. Stephen sat on the cushion, frozen and too afraid to speak.

"Please, you must stop screaming," the eyes said looking around frantically.

"Stay away from me!" Wendy yelled. Stephen watched Wendy as she scooted away from the velvet cushion. He turned back to the eyes, paranoid that they would move closer to him.

"Whoareyou?" Wendy asked breathlessly.

"Mary," the eyes said nervously.

"Hideaway?" asked Stephen.

"What?" replied Mary.

"Hideaway...is that your last name?"

"Duke," Mary answered.

"What?"

"My last name is Duke," said Mary. "I knew the Hideaways long ago. We lived in the same town. You know the Hideaways?"

"They're the reason we're here. They made

us come here to reverse the curse," Stephen cautiously explained. "You said you lived in the same town?"

"Correct."

"Duke," Stephen heard Wendy whisper to herself. She looked worried and her mouth hung open. "Like Sir Edward Duke?" Wendy finally asked.

Mary giggled a little. "Oh no, no, no...I'm not him. Certainly not."

Stephen sighed. He could feel the tension in his shoulders ease a little.

"I'm his wife," said Mary.

Stephen felt himself scooting away from Mary just as Wendy had done seconds earlier. He searched Mary's eyes for any signs of malevolence. He could find none. The blue in her eyes made her look serene and nurturing, unlike the icy, cold blue in Ronald's son's eyes.

"Please don't be afraid and don't make too much noise," Mary said, lowering her voice. "I can help you find him."

"Who?" asked Stephen. He thought that his question might've been dumb, but he hadn't had time to stop and think before he spoke.

"Sir Edward Duke. If the Hideaways sent you here, I can assure you that you're in the right place. I bet you *are* the ones meant to break the curse," Mary said excitedly. "How did you get here?"

"Her basement. There was this door and—"

"Through your very own house?" Mary said turning to Wendy. "You surely are the ones. Both of you. One boy and one girl."

"Do you mean that other kids have been here too?" Stephen asked Mary.

"Yes...you could say that. Children can't last very long here. You must hurry. You don't have much time. Too long here and you'll turn into nothing more than a pair of eyes."

"Too long?" Wendy asked with terror in her voice. "What's too long? We only have until tonight."

"I'm not quite sure what too long is," Mary answered. "No child has ever quite made it out successfully."

Stephen felt nostalgic. He *had* to get back home. What about *Dead Zombie Attack Part V* nights with Mark and Vince? What about his mom and dad and Matt? He wished he were back in Hinsdale where alternate universes and basements with wishmasters didn't exist.

"Why should we trust you? You're probably helping him," Stephen accused Mary. He had to admit, it seemed an unfair accusation given how nice Mary had been, but no one could be trusted.

As Mary started to speak, all appeared to grow even quieter. The flicker of the flames in the sconces didn't even seem to be as loud. They blazed quietly and low.

"I married Edward nearly two thousand years ago. He has never been the most charming man, but he was a wishmaster, and wives of wishmasters were always feared and well respected. One day, he left to attend a party. There were wishes to be granted, you know."

Stephen nodded thoughtlessly.

"I chose to stay at home that day, as I was meeting a couple of ladies for my monthly tea party. I was fixing my hair in the palace mirror when all of a sudden I couldn't see myself any longer. It was as if I'd disappeared without warning or a trace. I knew it had to be one of Edward's granted wishes. Sure enough, it was. When he got home, he explained to me, rather nonchalantly I may add, that he had turned the entire town into nothing more than a set of eyes."

"Did he ever become eyes too?" Stephen asked curiously.

"Wishmasters are immune to their own granted wishes. It just doesn't happen that way."

"Their wives aren't immune?" asked Wendy.

"No...we are not. Anyway," Mary continued, "he took pity on me and brought me here with him in his castle. The rest of the town, he set free in your world."

"In *our* world?" Wendy asked with her how-is-this-even-possible face.

Mary's eyes bobbed up and down like they were nodding yes.

"But," Stephen said, finally warming up to the blue in Mary's eyes, "why didn't he just unwish his wish?"

"What a wishmaster has wished for remains until one boy and one girl undo the curse," Mary explained. Her eyes turned to Stephen. "You are to help your friend here and when she feels as though she cannot go on, you must encourage her."

"What? No action?" Stephen asked, disappointed. He sank back in the cushion. This was his first real life adventure since *Dead Zombie Attack Part V*. He knew for a fact that you could not defeat a zombie, or a wishmaster, with encouragement. But here was Mary, insisting that he step back and watch and *encourage.* Reason number 7,948 why moving to Wally Heights sucked.

"Yes, dear. The girl makes the wish. Those are the rules," Mary said, staring at Stephen.

"I'm not really sure this is what I signed up for," Wendy said shyly.

"If you have been chosen for this, darling, you are braver than you think. You must conquer your fears to find Sir Edward Duke. Once you find him, you'll need to make a wish to break the curse."

Stephen started to hear whispers that grew louder. And screams. And shouts of laughter.

A sharp breeze blew by them, blowing two of the flames out.

"I have to go," Mary said in a panicked voice.

"But wait! Where are you going?" asked Wendy, just as panicked.

By this time, the screams and shouts had drawn closer and were unbearably loud.

Mary turned to Wendy. "Remember that you are brave and, whatever you do, don't be afraid!" she reminded her. As Mary floated toward one of the castle walls, she looked back and yelled, "And do excuse my manners. We'll chat about your names later." She turned toward the gray, rocky palace wall.

"Wait!!" Stephen yelled at Mary.

But it was too late. Mary was long gone.

CHAPTER 17

Stephen and Wendy frantically looked around for a place to hide as they heard the footsteps and laughter drawing closer, but there was nowhere to go.

Stephen grew so frightened that his vision blurred. He felt hot all over. First, another mysterious set of eyes had appeared, and now, something was approaching that even *the eyes* had been afraid of. He looked behind himself and up toward the sky for the door they had fallen through. There was no sign of anything above besides pure, undisturbed blackness.

Just ahead, Stephen saw a short horizontal wall sitting perpendicular to the castle wall. He rushed to take a spot behind the wall, silently waving Wendy along. He waited. He had not even run that fast and already he could feel himself growing sweaty and sticky.

"Do you hear that?" Wendy asked Stephen.

"Hear what?" Stephen asked, wiping his forehead.

"Listen," Wendy whispered.

Stephen could now hear a soft, faint cry in the distance. "I hear it," Stephen whispered back in amazement.

"Another kid?" asked Wendy.

"I don't know. Sounds like a boy."

"Why is he crying?" Wendy asked Stephen.

"How should I know?"

"Should we help?" Wendy asked, panicking.

Stephen didn't have an answer. He put his knees together and wrapped his arms around them. He buried his head in his knees to drown out all sound. But as subtle and soft as the boy's cries were, it was nearly impossible to ignore them. They rang repetitively like bells inside of his head. He swallowed hard to get rid of the lump that he felt forming in his throat.

Finally, Stephen rose to his feet and started toward the sound of the cries. Wendy followed. Stephen and Wendy walked for what seemed like miles, seeing only the hallway they had just left and the hallway they were headed toward. Neither of them spoke on the way.

The little boy's loud cries turned to softer whimpers.

"Hello?" Stephen called. "We can try to help you, but we don't know where you are... or where we are. Where are you?"

But the boy did not answer. Stephen

wondered if the boy had even heard him. With Wendy following, he crept further into the dark hallway. He shivered from the castle's cold air blowing on his wet back.

"Hello?" he whispered again.

Stephen thought that perhaps they should turn around. After all, the boy could be standing directly in front of them and neither he nor Wendy would know. Anything or anyone could be reaching to grab them—anything could be watching them.

It was hard for Stephen to move without growing dizzier by the second. He wiped his palms on his pants. Too afraid to reach out with his hands, he put his foot in front of him to make sure the path was clear.

"I think we're getting closer. I can hear him again," Wendy said.

"I don't know."

Stephen heard a rustling sound. His jaw shook. He reached in front of him to stop Wendy, stopping just short of gripping the skin on her back. Wendy screamed.

"Shhh!" Stephen reminded her.

"Was that you?" Wendy asked with terror in her voice.

"Who else? Be quiet!"

"Maybe it isn't such a good idea to reach for someone's back in the dark!" Wendy snapped.

"Did you hear that?" Stephen asked.

"Hear what?"

"A crinkly rustling sound. Like someone is moving around."

Stephen shook all over, desperately wanting a glass of ice-cold water and his warm, soft sheets back in Wally Heights. He even missed Matt.

A thick, uncomfortable tension filled the air.

"I think I hear someone coming. Quick, hide!" Wendy whispered. Stephen felt downright silly hiding in so much darkness. He crouched down and remained still.

Stephen heard heavy footsteps toward the entrance of the hallway. He hoped Wendy had been smart enough to crouch down just as he had. His breaths quickened before he decided it would be better to just stop breathing altogether. He could feel himself turning red, but he didn't care. He rubbed his palms against his pants.

Suddenly, Stephen saw a beam of light. And another one. Then there was a voice. A few. The beams danced frantically around the hallway. Stephen crouched even lower, hoping he wouldn't be seen. As the light beamed right past him, he could see it shine directly on Wendy who lay crouched on her side. And then, the other beam found Stephen.

He could feel a thick, muscular arm gripping him and lifting him into the air. The grasp was so tight he thought he might burst at the stomach. Stephen felt himself bouncing up and down. His dizziness increased as he tried to kick and bite the man. He thought he might throw up and in this case, he hoped he would. He could hear Wendy's screams in the background.

"Let me go!" Stephen managed to yell. But it was no use. The man carrying him was too strong. He imagined that his bites must've felt like small bird pecks to such a large adult.

The men walked toward the hallway that Stephen and Wendy had originally hidden in, and before long, Stephen and Wendy could feel themselves being hurled onto a hard, wet, muddy surface.

CHAPTER 18

Stephen lay on the cold, dirty concrete slab, tossing and turning. His hips ached with every roll to his opposite side. Wendy sat sulking in a corner, her arms wrapped tightly around her knees. Stephen got up and stood against a wall with his feet propped out in front of him. He closed his eyes.

"What are you doing?" asked Wendy.

"The floor hurts," Stephen said.

"Humans don't sleep standing up. Bats do."

Stephen ignored Wendy, continuing to stand against the wall sleeping.

"Oh, dear," said a familiar voice that didn't sound like Wendy's. Stephen opened his eyes. He flinched as he squinted at the eyes that watched him from the corner of the cell. His body shook—something he tried to hide by shoving his hands in his pockets. Could the Hideaways be visiting him outside of Wally

Heights? Had they been checking up on him to make sure he had adhered to their warning?

"Oh! Don't be afraid. It's me, Mary," said the eyes.

"Geez! Could you stop doing that? Maybe give us a warning or something first?" Stephen snapped, as he stood up straighter.

"Shhhhh! Please, keep your voice down," said Mary.

"Why are we here?" Stephen asked impatiently. "And what does sitting in an old, dirty place have to do with saving the Hideaways?"

"This is the holding cell where all of Edward's visitors stay...you can certainly see why we don't have very many visitors. Wendy, you must be sure to have your wish together. Edward will be expecting it now that he knows you're here."

Stephen sighed heavily. He had been so focused on getting to Sir Edward Duke that he had forgotten all about the wish.

Without warning, heavy footsteps stomped through the hallways. Stephen ran toward the door of the cell and looked out of its small window.

"Where'd she go?" Wendy shouted as she watched Mary's eyes vanish.

Stephen looked back at Wendy and then back out of the small window on the door. He would deal with Mary later. The footsteps that he heard seemed far more important.

Two large men walked past the window while looking straight ahead. Stephen banged on the window to get their attention, but it seemed to be no use. The men continued to walk stiffly past him as though they heard nothing.

Red-faced and frustrated, Stephen turned around to see Mary poignantly floating in the corner again.

"Why do you always do that?" Stephen asked, startled again by Mary.

"Please don't lose patience. We all need you," said Mary.

"We?" Wendy asked curiously.

"The people of Teafall! We've all got this nasty curse and, why, if the Hideaways found you and you can cure it...do you know what this means?" Mary said excitedly.

Stephen stared at Wendy, who still looked like she had seen a headless ghost, and then at Mary. Something in Mary's eyes looked desperate. It made Stephen feel powerful, even more than winning in *Dead Zombie Attack Part V* did.

"How long do we have to wait until we see Sir Edward Duke? We can't wait much longer," Stephen asked Mary with frustration in his voice.

"Well...I...I...the thing is...I don't really

know. It could be days, months, years, decades, centuries."

"Centuries! Those *things*—the Hideaways—could knock my whole family off in a century. I can't be here for centuries! I can't even afford to be here for a night," Stephen exploded.

"Centuries?" Wendy cut in, coming out of her somber mood. "We'll be dead in centuries!"

"I can't stay here for centuries! This was a bad idea. I have to go. We have to go. There has to be another way to help the Hideaways," Stephen said. He started to grow hot all over.

Panicked, Mary looked from Stephen to Wendy, and Wendy to Stephen. "I am begging you...we need your help. Please help us. Without you, we'll stay like this forever."

Stephen wasn't exactly sure, but he could have sworn he saw a small tear fall from Mary's eye and drop to the floor.

CHAPTER 19

Several hours after Mary had visited and informed him that he may possibly die an eleven-year-old prisoner in an evil, balding man's castle, Stephen realized that he was hungry. His stomach growled in anticipation of the morning's meal. His head ached terribly from lying on concrete slabs. Mary had been wrong if she thought that he would wait centuries to talk to Sir Edward Duke. There had to be a quicker way.

"When do you think they'll come for us?" Wendy asked as she wiped a dirt stain from her face. She looked horrible, like she had already been there for months.

"I don't know. Soon, I hope. Has to be soon." Stephen thought about Vince and Mark and how they acted like they half believed him. *Dead Zombie Attack Part V* had never seemed quite as real as it did now.

Suddenly, Stephen heard a loud creak. The oversized room door opened.

"Sir Edward Duke is ready to receive you

now," a deep male voice said. But neither Stephen nor Wendy moved. Stephen wondered what or who had opened the door.

The door squeaked a little more as it swung back farther. All was quiet inside the castle. Stephen and Wendy lifted themselves from the floor and walked toward the door.

When they stepped outside, no one was there.

"Come on," said Stephen motioning to Wendy who lagged behind.

"Which way do we go?" Wendy asked, following closer behind Stephen.

"It looks like there's only one way." Sure enough, all of the castle pathways had become obsolete. There was one path straight ahead of them.

"I'm not so sure about this," said Wendy, wiping her face with her arm.

"We have to go. I don't see any other option unless you want to go back to that room we were just in."

Wendy reluctantly shuffled closer to Stephen. They both turned sideways and walked down the narrow path, their backs against the wall and their hands planted firmly against it.

Stephen could feel his breathing start to change. His breaths were short and forced. His hands trembled terribly and his knees knocked together with each sidestep he took.

He couldn't have been more relieved to see the small, faintly lit exit ahead of them.

One by one, they squeezed through the exit, the concrete walls of the pathway scraping their arms as they passed through.

Straight ahead of them were two identical tall, plain, wooden doors set against blackness. Each door had red lettering above it: "Long way" was written over the door to the left and "Shortcut" over the other.

"Do you hear that?" Wendy whispered.

"Hear what?"

"Listen," Wendy urged him.

Stephen was still. He listened closely. Barking. The sound was vague, but powerful. The roars and barks sounded as though they were coming from behind the shortcut door.

"Barks," Stephen concluded out loud.

"It's coming from over there," Wendy said as she pointed to the door on the right. She swallowed hard. "Let's choose the one on the left," she said without hesitation.

"But that one says 'long way.' Long could mean forever in here," Stephen protested.

"Did you not hear the dogs behind the shortcut door? To me, forever sounds a whole lot better than winding up as dog food."

"Sir Edward Duke must be trying to chase us away. We can't let him. Maybe we can somehow make it past the dogs. Or maybe it's a trick and there really aren't any dogs."

"How could you even think it's a good idea for us to open a door full of hungry...angry... *barking* dogs?"

"Dogs don't eat people," Stephen said matter-of-factly.

"Werewolf dogs do," Wendy said defiantly.

"Who said anything about werewolves?" Stephen asked, confused.

"We're in another world saving pairs of eyes. Anything is possible, right? Besides, those don't sound like regular barks."

"You don't say," Stephen joked. He laughed, but he knew Wendy was right. They had seen just about everything. Werewolf dogs didn't sound too far-fetched. Stephen held his stomach tightly, ignoring the knot that was forming.

He remembered Mary's pleas from earlier. Her words echoed like sounds in an empty auditorium: *"Help us."* Stephen did not know Mary well, and he certainly had not known her for very long, but there was something innocent about her. She had seemed so genuine and helpless. He had to help. "We gotta choose the shortcut door," Stephen said, hiding his own fear behind his brave words.

"Okay, I'll see you in a few years," Wendy said as she rushed over to the "Long way" door.

Stephen grabbed her by the arm. "No, don't

do it! We have to face our fears. We're here for a reason."

"All thanks to you!" Wendy shouted. She screamed in frustration. The barks grew louder. Stephen could tell that the dogs sensed their presence. He blinked hard as sweat dropped into his eyes. He paced back and forth as the dogs barked viciously. He pictured strong, thick-necked wolves with their noses against the door, salivating and sniffing at him and Wendy.

"What are you afraid of? Dogs or werewolves?" asked Stephen.

"Werewolf dogs," Wendy said through her tears.

Stephen paused and looked toward the "shortcut" door. If this was a test of their fears, he knew that the drooling, sharp-fanged werewolf dogs that he had pictured were indeed on the other side of the door on the right.

CHAPTER 20

"There's no time. We have to hurry," Stephen urged Wendy.

"Does time even exist here?" Wendy asked.

Stephen imagined the Hideaways watching him at night angrily while they made things fly and float and strike him. He pictured the Hideaways gingerly sliding the covers off of him while he slept and dragging him by the feet to the McCallister house while his nails scraped across his wooden floor. What would the Hideaways do to him if he didn't finish his mission? If *they* didn't finish? "I don't know. I just have a feeling that we shouldn't lollygag," he finally said.

He hesitantly looked back at Wendy as he walked toward the door on the right. He could hear the roars on the other side of the door grow louder as he drew closer. He placed his hand on the cold, small black doorknob. His breaths were short sighs.

He stood for a minute staring at the door,

listening to the roars of what he thought may very well be the last sounds he would ever hear.

With every ounce of might, Stephen flung the door wide open. There was silence and something that he felt he could never grow accustomed to again since meeting the Hideaways: complete darkness.

"What now?" Wendy asked frantically.

"I don't know."

"Can you hear the dogs?" she asked.

"I can't hear anything."

Both children looked beyond the doorway again and stared at the darkness as though something noisy would come out of it, but the barking had left.

"We gotta go through," Stephen said.

Wendy looked at Stephen fearfully through her tears.

"It's the only way home. That other door looks like a trap," he said.

"But what if this one is a trap?"

"I guess we'll find that out," Stephen said to Wendy.

"Aren't you even a little afraid?" she asked.

"No," Stephen said with his nose turned in the air.

Wendy shook her head as though she didn't believe Stephen. "I wanna go home. No. As a matter of fact, I wanted to *STAY* home. This whole thing was your idea!"

"Was it my idea, *really*?" Stephen said.

Wendy didn't reply.

"C'mon, let's go," yelled Stephen.

Wendy filled her cheeks with air and walked sluggishly toward Stephen and the doorway.

Stephen stepped into the doorway first, his legs shaking and his hands slippery. Wendy stepped close in behind him.

Stephen raised his hand in front of him, but could not see it. He looked behind. He couldn't tell if the door had disappeared or if darkness had overwhelmed it. Either way, it was no longer open and he knew that turning back was no longer an option.

"Is there a candle or a lantern anywhere?" Wendy asked.

"I don't think so. We'll just have to hurry and make it through."

"Make it through to where?" asked Wendy.

"I don't know, but the longer we spend talking about it, the longer it'll take to get home."

Stephen sighed as he continued to walk forward with Wendy. There was a strange sound every time they stepped. It reminded Stephen of the sound autumn leaves made when they crunched underneath his foot, but it didn't smell like outside. In fact, he hadn't smelled much of anything at all besides the cold air that zoomed up his nostrils with every deep breath he took. He reached his hands in front of him again and touched nothing. It seemed they were in a wide, open space. The uncomfortable chill in the air made Stephen even more afraid.

He heard a stirring in the distance. And then, he saw it: the very thing that had propelled them to come there. The whites of eyeballs staring from one side of the room. And they seemed to be walking forward cautiously. Stephen grew hot and itchy. The eyes didn't notice them. At least, Stephen didn't think they did. As they got closer to a couple of the eyeballs, he could hear mumbles and shouts. They all sounded like children.

"I don't wanna be here!" cried one voice.

"I'm so scared. Please help!" cried another.

"I don't know what to do. I don't know where to go!"

One by one, voices uttered laments and pleas for help.

"We should've chosen the other door! I knew it!" yelled Wendy.

"Be quiet! Do you want one of them to hear us?" Stephen warned.

Suddenly, Stephen looked beside him and screamed in terror. A large pair of eyeballs had gotten so close to him that he could feel an extra set of short breaths. The eyes widened as they stared at Stephen.

"Please help," a young girl's voice pleaded.

CHAPTER 21

Stephen screamed louder than he had intended to. He wondered if the other eyeballs would come to get him too. He grabbed for Wendy, who stood frozen at the other side of him. He tugged frantically and desperately at her sleeve. But she would not, and probably could not, move. Stephen screamed loudly again.

"Get back!" he yelled, out of breath.

He could hear the young girl crying softly. "I just need your help, someone's help, anybody, just help," she mumbled. He again thought he saw a tear drop. It was the second time he had ever seen such a thing from the eyes. He wondered if the Hideaways cried, too.

"We're not falling for that again. We can't help you. Go away," he said, shooing the girl away.

"Please...I don't know where I am. I chose the wrong door! Please!"

A lump formed in Stephen's throat. He could hardly utter his next words without his eyes watering. "What do you mean you chose the wrong door?" he asked.

"I don't know. It sounds silly. I chose the short way. There were these two doors and I thought that choosing the short way would be smarter...and obviously faster. Can you help me? Please..."

"Two doors?" Stephen asked. He began to get dizzy all over again. It had never occurred to him that the shortcut door could be the wrong door.

Wendy echoed Stephen. "Wrong door? What do you mean you chose the wrong door?"

"Oh, none of it is important now. It's all hopeless. All of this because of some stupid curse I tried to help cure. I don't care if I ever see that ugly, miserable, little man! I just want to find my way home. Can you help me?" the girl asked, her innocent-looking eyes twinkling.

"I'm sorry...I don't think we can. We don't know much about where we are either," Stephen answered.

The eyes moved up and down as though nodding solemnly. He watched as the eyes turned away from him and walked toward the rest.

"I think we chose the wrong door," Stephen said dreadfully, watching the eyeballs walk away.

"I told you we should have picked the other one," Wendy said.

"Maybe it's not too late. We haven't come that far. Maybe we can still go back," he said, half-believing himself.

Stephen turned around only to see another set of eyes. He took a step back. Why were the eyes starting to surround him?

"It's me!" the eyes said.

"Me, who?" Wendy asked, also backing away.

"Oh dear...I didn't mean to frighten you. It's Mary, from earlier. Please don't be alarmed."

"Why do you keep popping up like that? It's unsettling," said Stephen.

"We picked the wrong door. Please help us," said Wendy. She sounded almost as desperate as the eyes that they had just talked to.

"Are you running because you're afraid? Please don't stop now. You are closer than you think. Edward would love it if you just stopped like all the rest."

"You just saw that girl...those eyes, right? She came here and said she picked the wrong door," explained Stephen.

"Well...so?" Mary asked.

"She sounded like she had been here for a while," Wendy added.

"Yeah, I thought this was supposed to be the shortcut. Are you going to help us out of here?" Stephen demanded. "And what kind of people are these anyway? Are *they* Hideaways?"

Mary shook her head no and stretched her hand toward the other wandering eyeballs. "These are all children who've come here to stop the curse, just like you."

"Living people?" Wendy asked.

Mary laughed. "Yes. Living ones. They, too, have come to see Sir Edward Duke, but their fear won't let them move on from this place. They've all been here so long that they've turned into the very affliction they were trying to cure."

"How long have they been here?" asked Wendy.

"Some for hours, some for days, some for years," Mary answered. "But you two...you're so brave. You can cure us all...I know you can."

"I just want to cure this curse and get out of here! What do we need to do?" Stephen asked. He was growing exhausted with the entire situation and his stomach still ached with hunger.

"Keep going. Don't run. Well, not yet, at least. Face your fears and you'll be in Sir Edward Duke's presence soon enough. But please, whatever you do, do not give up." With that, Mary disappeared into the darkness that she had materialized from.

The children turned and walked toward the

eyeballs again. But as Stephen walked with Wendy through crowds of "help me please" and "how do I get out of here" laments, he soon saw why no one else had bothered to move forward. He stopped, unable to think, move, or breathe.

CHAPTER 22

"We have to run. It's the only way through," Stephen said.

Wendy's logical mind told her that Stephen was perhaps right, but her body felt like it might collapse if she so much as tried to take a step forward. "I can't. I can't move," Wendy said as she stiffened with her hands to her side.

She stared at the wolves in front of her and Stephen. They didn't look like ordinary wolves, not that she had seen any in person. On all fours, they had nearly come up to Wendy's waist. Their red eyes illuminated slivers of silky silver fur. They snarled their lips up at the children to show their teeth. Saliva dripped down their long, white fangs.

"There are only two of them," said Stephen.

"Two too many," Wendy shot back. She hated the way Stephen tried to act brave. He had probably been more scared than she was.

"You've got to make a run for it," Stephen urged. "On the count of three, go. Ready?"

"Me? What? No! I can't do this! You're crazy!" Stephen was crazy if he thought that she was about to run past werewolf-looking dogs all by herself.

"You're the one that has to make the wish. You have to go," Stephen insisted.

"What about you?" Wendy asked desperately.

"I'll be fine. Just pretend like you're wandering like the rest of them. Pretend you're a Hideaway or something. Wander first and then run past. Don't start off running or they'll come after you. I'll distract them."

"How on earth are you going to distract wolves? I can't just leave you here!" The wolf on the right snarled at Wendy. A large blob of the wolf's drool dripped to the floor.

"We don't have much time. Just go. I'll meet up with you. I promise."

Wendy couldn't speak. She had never had someone fight off wolves for her.

"Count of three," Stephen said.

Wendy nodded yes.

"One."

The wolf closest to Wendy showed more of its teeth as though it was warning her to stay away.

"Two."

The wolf on the left let out a long vicious howl. The other wolf joined in. They both stared at the dark ceiling, howling away any escapees.

"Three. Go. Wander away and then run," yelled Stephen. "I'll be right there. I promise. Go."

Wendy walked away from Stephen, glancing back occasionally. "Come here, boy," she heard Stephen say as he pulled something out of his pocket. She watched as the wolves kept their eyes on something that Stephen held out in front of him.

Wendy walked as far away from Stephen as she could, trying to figure out what lay ahead. But it was too dark. It was also too risky not to run now. Wendy knew from her science class that wolves didn't have the longest attention span. A few more seconds and the wolves would start to notice her again.

She walked a little faster...and faster...and faster until, finally, she ran past the wolves that stared at Stephen with a hungry look in their eyes.

CHAPTER 23

Even as Stephen held the five-day-old, pocket lint-filled beef jerky bravely, his hands shook. He watched the wolves as they glared at him, growling and jerking toward him occasionally. He gripped the beef jerky with everything he had, careful not to drop it in front of the red-eyed wolves.

His vision blurred as he began to get lightheaded. Wendy had successfully run past the wolves. Now she would finally get to make her wish in front of Sir Edward Duke. But how would he escape? Where was Mary now when he needed her?

Stephen stepped back and away from the wolves. They didn't bother to follow him. He took another small step back. The wolves looked a little more disinterested. One more step back and they no longer showed Stephen their teeth.

The wolves really had been guarding *something*. Stephen inched toward the wolves again, the beef jerky shaking violently in his hands. He focused on not falling forward as his legs wobbled. As he drew close to them, the wolves began to show their long, sharp teeth again to warn him. When he had finally gotten as close as the wolves would let him, he looked into their eyes. They looked furious and partly evil. Their growls were so deep and guttural that Stephen could almost feel the vibration of them from where he stood.

He had to do something quick. Maybe the answer had been to distract them. It had to be. There was no other way. He raised his hand and with all the might that he could muster, he threw the dirty piece of beef jerky behind the wolves. Both wolves turned to look at the jerky, and one of them even ran to get it, its bushy silver tail high in the air. Stephen started past the distracted wolves, but the wolf on the right who hadn't run for the beef jerky stopped him. It growled the biggest and most ferocious growl that it had let out yet—one that caught the attention of the other children around. Stephen backed away from the wolves, keeping his eyes on them the entire time.

"What are you doing?" Stephen heard a voice ask. "You're going to get killed!"

"Isn't it better to be here than be dead?" he heard another voice ask.

Voices rang out from all around him, trying to convince him that he was making a mistake in trying to escape. "Come over here. We can find another way." "I thought just like you when I first got here." "He's going to be wolf meat!"

Stephen covered his ears and stared at the wolves in anger. He *had* to get past. He could not, and would not, be stuck. But then he thought of something. Something that he might not have otherwise thought about in a time like this. Maybe he could have passed the zombie attack in level 12 of *Dead Zombie Attack Part V* had Vince and Mark gone with him up to the zombie attack line. Maybe the zombies didn't have as much of a chance if it were three of them instead of just him. Perhaps he had gone about it all wrong.

He took his hands off of his ears and looked behind himself at the sea of eyes. Maybe, just maybe, if they all banded together, the wolves would be helpless. After all, the wolves would not be able to get *everybody.*

"Hey!" Stephen said to the eyes of the children as he held his hands up. "I think I have a plan."

"What plan?" "It's hopeless!" he heard their voices ring out.

"It's not hopeless," Stephen protested. "Hear me out."

The eyes remained silent, though some had already clearly lost interest as they looked in the distance away from Stephen.

"We can all work together to distract these wolves. They may be strong, but they're not that smart. The more of us there are, the harder it'll be for them to concentrate. And besides, how can they bite you if the rest of you can't be seen? What can they do to you?" Stephen asked.

"I'm not willing to find out!" he heard a young boy's voice cry out. The other eyes murmured in agreement.

"Okay, fine. You don't have to escape, but please at least do me this favor. Help me. I'm trying to cure the curse that Sir Edward Duke put on the town of Teafall and my friend is back there making a wish as we speak. Well... actually, I don't know if she made it back there. I'm not even sure she's safe. You've got to help me help her!" Stephen pleaded.

The eyes did not comment.

"Who knows? Maybe I can even help you guys if I can cure the curse," Stephen said desperately.

The eyes were still silent. Finally Stephen heard, "What do we have to do?"

Stephen breathed a sigh. "All you have to do is walk up there with me and I'll run across," he said, pointing toward the wolves. "You don't have to run with me, but you can."

"I'm not running anywhere!" a voice said.

"He'll be wolf meat!" said another.

"You don't have to run across," Stephen

repeated. "Two wolves can't possibly watch *all* of us. I will run—all you guys have to do is walk up to the line. Please. My friend and I both need your help."

There was a long pause, and for a second, Stephen thought his idea wouldn't work. The eyes had all seemed to be happily paralyzed by fear. But then, one of the eyes came walking toward him.

He watched in fearful anticipation as the eyes stared at him as they got closer. They walked directly past Stephen and toward the line. And then a few more walked. As some of the eyes got closer to the wolves, the animals growled furiously, curling their lips upward to show their teeth. Of course not all eyes were onboard with the plan. A few of them stayed behind, murmuring complaints about becoming wolf meat.

Stephen was grateful for the few that did march toward the wolves. As he marched over to meet them, the chill in the air seemed more real than it ever had. He rubbed his left arm, feeling lines of goose bumps.

Stephen knew it was time. If he didn't try to run now, he likely never would. He breathed a deep sigh, looking at the wolves as he positioned his feet to sprint. He counted in his head. On the count of three, he would make a run for it.

One.

Two.

Before he could hit the number three, Stephen ran over the invisible line with an electric burst of energy. He was a moving blur, and only when he could no longer feel the animals' massive presence and hot breath in the air, did he realize that he had gotten past the wolves. He ran until his chest burned so badly that he was sure his ribcage was on fire.

Without warning, Stephen felt something violently tug at his pant leg. He fell face-first onto the cold, tile floor. The pain had not been much. Besides a throbbing in his nose, Stephen felt fine. He hadn't been able to see a lot of what happened, but he knew his pants had to be ripped from the sound that he heard. Stephen rolled over onto his back only to see the two large wolves breathing over him anxiously. It even looked like they were smiling. Sweat streamed down his face. He hoped the wolves would not want to eat him for it.

He wanted to scream for help, but his throat ached from dryness. He was sure that even after he opened his mouth, nothing would come out. Where were the other kids? The eyes? Would they let him become wolf meat? Would they just let him die?

The room began to spin. Nothing else mattered but the two hungry-looking wolves looming over him. Now more than ever, Stephen felt like he needed to concentrate on them. He wanted to look into their red, glowing eyes in the hopes that somehow, some way, he could predict the moment right before he was to become wolf meat.

The wolves looked like they were challenging him—like they took pleasure in listening to the quick thumps in his chest. The truth was, all of the other kids could have run past the wolves at this very moment. Stephen was sure that the creatures would be too happy to have him for lunch to care.

One of the wolves placed a paw on Stephen's chest. It felt like the same weight as a bowling ball—heavier than he expected. He knew at least one wolf knew how scared he was now. The wolf's large, warm paw practically swallowed his heartbeat; each rough thud gave it energy.

Something thicker than sweat and tears trickled down to his lips. He reached up with his hands and touched his face. His fingertips were red with blood. He stared frantically at the wolves, who seemed to be amused that he had just discovered he was bleeding. They closed in on him, hovering like vultures.

"Hey! Over here! Hey you!" Stephen heard a girl's voice say.

"Hey! Yoo hoo!" the voice said again. The wolves whipped their necks toward the sound.

Stephen wished that he could run to the voice, but the wolves had pinned him down good. "Go fetch!" he heard the voice say. The wolves ran off into the distance.

"Get up! Run! Run, Stephen!" the voice shouted once the wolves ran away. "Hurry up!"

Stephen hopped up as though he had not just fallen moments earlier and darted toward the area the wolves had been protecting. His legs ached from running so fast. He hoped they would not give out. The wolves were nowhere in sight, but that did not mean that things would stay that way for very long.

Ignoring the burn in his legs and the fact that it hurt to breathe, he continued to run until the image in the distance became much clearer. It was Wendy. She held open a large door, motioning for Stephen to run inside.

CHAPTER 24

Stephen slipped through the crack of the door just before Wendy frantically slammed it behind him. He reached out and wrapped his arms around her. After a few seconds, she hugged him back. He couldn't blame her for being hesitant. *He* had barely even known that he would hug her.

"Are you okay?" Wendy said as she stepped back awkwardly and stared at the tear in the leg of Stephen's pants.

Stephen nodded yes. He focused his attention on the two metal handprint molds that sat mounted against the plain brick wall in front of him. He looked to the left and right of the molds. Nothing appeared to be in the narrowed hallway but wall, and both directions seemed to lead nowhere.

"Well, did they get you? Are you bleeding?" asked Wendy.

"No, just my face...or my nose. I'm fine. Really," Stephen said, still staring curiously at the wall molds. "Thanks for helping me back there. You were supposed to be going to make your wish," he said finally looking at Wendy.

"I couldn't have if I wanted to," answered Wendy. She pointed at the hand molds on the wall. "I think it's for two people. One of the hand imprints looks bigger than the other."

"Oh," said Stephen.

"And plus," Wendy started again, "I couldn't just leave you behind."

"What did you do?" asked Stephen. "How did you get those wolves to go away?"

"I threw a couple of balls," Wendy answered casually.

"That's it? How did you know it would work?"

"Natural dog instinct, I guess," she said.

"Where'd the balls come from?"

"They were here when I stepped inside of the door," Wendy said. She used her hand to smooth her hair back into a neater ponytail.

"You're welcome," a woman's voice said.

Fear welled up inside of Stephen. He looked around frantically and saw Mary's big, blue eyes. His shoulders relaxed a little.

"You put the balls there?" Wendy asked.

"I sure did. And I knew you'd be just smart enough to figure things out," said Mary. Wendy blushed sheepishly as if no one had ever paid her a compliment before.

"Are we supposed to put our hands in

there?" Stephen asked Mary, pointing at the metal molds on the wall.

"Yes. You must. It is the only way you'll get in to see Sir Edward Duke."

"Get in where?" Stephen asked.

"Yea," Wendy agreed, "this just looks like all wall. Is there a door somewhere?"

"You'll see," said Mary in a proud voice. "The time has come. You have made it farther than most people have made it."

"*Most* people?" asked Stephen. "What happened to the rest?"

Mary laughed. "Always one for detail, aren't you, little one? Go on now. It's time. Show him that you're as fearless as he once was when he turned us all into *this*."

"Wait, but—" Stephen protested.

"Go get him," said Mary. Her eyes disappeared before he could ask anything else.

"I guess we put our hands in here?" Stephen said, inching closer to the mold.

"Are you sure about this?" asked Wendy.

"You're kidding me, right?" Stephen said with a chuckle.

"What?"

"We've come all this way. We got dropped hundreds of feet into a world we know nothing about, slept in a prison, fought off wolves, and you're still worried?"

"That's exactly why I *am* worried," said Wendy. "Who knows what's behind this wall?"

"I'm pretty sure it can't be anything worse than what we've been through," said Stephen.

He walked over to the wall and placed his hand in the bigger mold. He had expected the metal to feel cold against his hand, but instead it felt warm—almost like it had been waiting for him. He stared at his hand, waiting for something to happen, but nothing did.

Wendy giggled.

"What?" Stephen asked defensively.

"I think your hand is in the wrong place," she said, pointing at the hand imprint that swallowed Stephen's hand. The imprint's long fingers stretched far beyond Stephen's short, skinny fingers.

"Are you ready to go make this wish or not?" Stephen snapped as he moved his hand to the smaller mold. It was also warm and a much better fit.

Still giggling softly to herself, Wendy walked up to the larger hand imprint and placed her long, skinny fingers inside of it.

Without warning, the wall began to shake and rumble like an earthquake was cracking it apart. Stephen planted his hands against the wall behind him. He covered his ears, but he heard the loud, growling rumble just the same.

"What did you do!" Stephen shouted at Wendy over the noise.

"I didn't do anything! What did *you* do?" Wendy yelled back.

The wall in front of them continued to chip away and break apart. Small, red brick crumbles fell at Stephen's feet.

When the front layer of the wall collapsed, it revealed a dull, golden door that sat against a brick wall that looked like the first. The door was so tall that neither Stephen nor Wendy could reach its high, bronze-colored doorknob.

"This has to be it," Stephen said aloud.

"How do you figure?" asked Wendy.

Stephen couldn't answer. He was too in awe of the tall, golden door. It looked ancient. Scratches and dents covered its front side. The color in it had faded. The knob on it was dull. Stephen had never been *this* close to a wishmaster. He wondered what was beyond the door.

"How are we going to get to that doorknob? You can stand on my shoulders," Wendy offered.

"I think you standing on *my* shoulders might work a little better," said Stephen.

Wendy shrugged. Stephen stood against the door right underneath the small doorknob and laced his fingers together, waiting on Wendy to put her long foot on top of them.

Wendy pushed her foot down on Stephen's hands. He wanted to stumble back a little from the sharp sting of her weight, but he stood firm, pretending that Wendy was as short as him and weighed next to nothing. Stephen prepared himself as he felt her starting to climb onto his shoulders.

He stood closer to the golden door to balance the weight of her against him. The minute he felt her step onto his shoulders, he could not pretend anymore. He felt like a kitten giving an ostrich a ride—though he would never admit it to Wendy.

"Hurry up," Stephen said as he held his hands firmly at his sides.

Wendy grunted as though she was having trouble with something.

"What are you doing up there?" Stephen struggled to concentrate on the wall ahead instead of the one hundred-odd pounds that stood on him.

One last loud grunt from Wendy and they were toppling to the floor, Wendy's legs tangled with Stephen. The big golden door creaked open slowly.

CHAPTER 25

Everything that Stephen or Wendy could have ever wanted was inside the small room, which to Stephen, resembled a cave. In one corner, at least ten big-screen TVs sat on top of mounds of golden bars. The room was covered in video games, microscopes, laptops, fancy cell phones, stuffed animals, tablets, and one hundred-dollar bills. Coins and gold and more bills sat beneath it all.

A man whose width covered the sides of his throne sat grinning, looking toward the doorway like he had been expecting someone. A small, square-shaped swimming pool sat in front of the throne, its bright red waters swishing back and forth as though something swam about.

"Ahhhh, so nice of you to join me," the man said in a nasally, mischievous voice. His smile grew wider. Those crooked, square, yellowed teeth, that bulging belly, the shiny big bald spot in the middle of his head, that voice. Stephen knew the man had to be Sir Edward Duke.

Stephen nudged Wendy, anxious to let her know they were standing in front of a real wishmaster. *The* wishmaster that was responsible for the Hideaway curse and the curse on all of the children in the castle.

"I know," Wendy said to Stephen the second time he nudged her. He hadn't looked over at her to see her expression, but Stephen could tell by the sound of her voice that she was standing stiffly, like him. He had no time to concentrate on much else besides holding his breath. He had heard one time that it made your heart beat slower, which made you calmer. Sweat slid down his nose and off the tip. A cool breeze blew through his wet, matted hair.

"Stephen," Sir Edward Duke said, smiling at Stephen from about twenty feet away, "she's a smart girl. She can figure out who I am." Sir Edward Duke turned to Wendy, who was now shaking and white with fear. "Can't you, dear?" he asked her.

Wendy stared at Sir Edward Duke daringly, but didn't answer.

"Can I trouble you for something?" Sir Edward Duke asked, leaning forward in his chair. His long black robe wrinkled, getting caught in the creases underneath his stomach.

Stephen stepped forward toward Sir

Edward Duke. A loud roar that echoed off the cave-like walls stopped him in his tracks. He felt the blood rushing to his face. His breaths were short and staccato again. He hadn't exactly known what was in Sir Edward Duke's swimming pool, but he now saw rows and rows of teeth poking through the moving, red waters.

"Ah, ah, ahhhh. Be careful, there. You can't quite throw a ball at this one, can you?" Sir Edward Duke said, motioning toward the waters and staring at Wendy.

"It's a fake!" Stephen heard a woman's voice say. Sir Edward Duke looked equally surprised. He looked around frantically to see where the voice came from.

"It's a fake!" the voice repeated.

Stephen looked to the left of Sir Edward Duke at a pair of big, blue eyes. He'd recognize those eyes anywhere. "Mary," he said to himself. Wendy, who looked more courageous and more ready to go home than she ever had, stood with her fists clenched.

"Edward, don't you ever try any new tricks? Honestly, you've had that same fake roaring goldfish for hundreds of years now," Mary said, looking at Sir Edward Duke. She turned to the children. "He's afraid of real animals. Fish and sharks included." She faced Sir Edward Duke again. "These children have earned their right to make a wish! They've made it here fair and square."

"Enough!" Sir Edward Duke yelled, slamming his thick hand against the golden throne.

"Go on and make your wish, Wendy. Don't be afraid. Don't let him try to scare—" Mary's voice cut off abruptly. Stephen watched as Mary's eyes continued to move as though she was talking, but all that escaped her was silence.

"Hey, you can't do that!" Wendy said angrily.

"I can do whatever I want. She's *my* wife!" Sir Edward Duke yelled. "Why have you come to see me?"

"You know why we're here," Stephen said, refusing to step toward the wishmaster again. "We want to make a wish!"

"And just who sent you here?" asked Sir Edward Duke.

"The Hideaways," Stephen answered before he knew it.

"The Hideaways?" Sir Edward Duke asked as though he was surprised by the answer.

Stephen stared at him sternly.

"Very well. Let me grant you one more wish first. Anything you want! Anything in the whole wide world is yours. Just one wish and then you can make your wish for the Hideaways," said Sir Edward Duke.

"No, it's not going to work! We came here to make our wish and that's what we're going to do!" Stephen shouted.

"Really? You're turning anything in the whole wide world down? Even all the money or gold or *video games* in the world?" asked Sir Edward Duke.

"Yes!" yelled Stephen.

"Wendy?" Sir Edward Duke called as he glared at her.

Hesitating, Wendy stood staring at Sir Edward Duke.

"Wendy, no!" Stephen shouted.

He looked over at Mary, who still could not speak. She sat off to the side of Sir Edward Duke, her eyes growing bigger at Wendy.

"Wendy," Stephen said as he put his hand on her shoulder. "Think about this. It's a trick. Remember Ronald's vision. Remember what Sir Edward Duke did to the Hideaways. Don't do it!" Mary's eyes bobbed up and down in agreement.

"I wish," Wendy started.

"No!"

"Yes? Yeeeeessssss?" Sir Edward Duke said, leaning in closer to hear Wendy clearly.

"Wendy, stop!"

"I wish," she said again with her fists still clenched, "that the curse that you put on the people in Teafall was broken and that every Hideaway and pair of eyes was a normal human being like the rest of us."

Just as the brick wall hiding the tall door had crumbled, the floor now broke apart into little pieces. Shiny golden coins fell through the cracks. Pieces of rock fell from the ceiling and around the children. TV screens cracked; golden coins and jewelry clanked; small rocks pushed in the faces of stuffed animals.

Sir Edward Duke's throne rumbled as he yelled, "Get out! All of you! Get out! Mutts!"

Grabbing Wendy by the arm, Stephen ran toward the doorway behind him. He darted through the cracked door, pulling Wendy roughly. It closed promptly behind them.

Once they were outside of the door, Stephen noticed someone on the floor to his right. There sat a beautiful woman with skin as smooth as silk and a cute, pointy nose. She wore her pale, blonde hair in what looked like a big and tall bun. Her dress looked very similar to what Stephen had seen when Ronald told his story: long and puffy on the bottom and slim-fitting on the top. A long piece of silver tape was splashed across her mouth. Stephen ripped it off and stared into the woman's large blue eyes.

"Oh dear!" the woman exclaimed as Stephen ripped the tape off. She patted the area around her mouth.

"Mary?" Wendy asked, amazed.

"Yes, yes, it's me!" Mary said excitedly. "You can see me?"

Stephen and Wendy nodded yes at the same time.

"Why, why, why, that means—"

"It worked!" Stephen yelled, finishing Mary's sentence. For the first time in hours, he could feel the tension leaving his back. In fact, he felt pretty good. Almost like he had run a marathon and come out first place—only even better.

"Oh, I don't know how to thank you enough. You did it!" Mary exclaimed as Stephen helped her off of the floor.

"We did it," Stephen said as he looked at an excited Wendy.

"We did it," Wendy said to herself softly.

"But wait, this means...the Hideaways! They're cured too!" Stephen pointed out.

"Oh, thank you," Mary said, hugging Stephen and Wendy at the same time. Stephen was grateful that she didn't feel cold. After all, she was technically hundreds of years old.

"You're welcome. It was no trouble. Really," Stephen said, bashfully staring at Mary's flushed cheeks. Wendy nodded in agreement.

"You must go back home now. Now that you've made your wish, you no longer need to be here," Mary explained.

"But what about you?" asked Wendy.

"Oh, I'll be fine. I've survived all these

years. Although, I must say, I do feel a familiar growling in my stomach. I'll have to search for some food around here. Food! Imagine that! I'm hungry!" Mary exclaimed as she laughed.

She put her small, slender hands on Stephen's and Wendy's shoulders and pointed to a barren, black hole in front of them.

"That is your way home," Mary said, looking at the hole.

Stephen looked at it, confused. "That hasn't been there the whole time, has it?" he asked.

Mary giggled. "No, my dear, it hasn't. Your mission here is finished. It is time for you to go home now."

"Thank you," Wendy said awkwardly.

"Yeah, thanks," said Stephen. Part of him had almost been sad to walk through the hole to go home, but a much larger part of him knew this was a time for celebration. The Hideaways could no longer do anything to him or his family. Nothing would watch him.

"Go on," Mary said sadly as she nudged the children toward the hole.

"We can always visit you, right?" Stephen said, staring at Mary expectantly.

"I don't quite think this would be the ideal vacation spot for children, but I'll tell you what..." Mary reached both hands behind her neck and unlatched a small silver locket. She opened the locket and looked inside its

172

tiny mirror. "I can see myself in it," she said proudly. She held the locket out to Wendy, who looked reluctant to accept. "This is now yours. Something to remember me by so you'll never have to visit this horrible place again." She smiled. "Go on, take it," she said to Wendy.

"Thank you; it's beautiful!" said Wendy. She bowed her head before looking up again. "Thank you."

"Now go, go, go!" Mary yelled playfully.

The children smiled and walked toward the black hole. They were sucked through like dust bunnies to a vacuum hose. Stephen hoped that Wendy held the fist with Mary's locket in it tightly.

CHAPTER 26

Stephen lay on his back, his elbows propped against the concrete floor, looking at the small door. It had been cracked a little until Wendy closed it gently. He watched as Wendy stood next to the door. She looked wild and untamed like she had just skydived. Stephen was glad to see the familiar sight of Wendy's red lawnmower sitting peacefully in the middle of the basement floor.

"We're back at your house?" a disoriented Stephen asked Wendy.

"I think so?" Wendy said, sounding unsure of her own answer.

"What just happened?" asked Stephen. His face felt chilly and rigid like all of the color had been drained from it.

"I don't know."

"My head hurts," Stephen said, rubbing his hand against his head. He looked down at the tear in his pants leg, remembering the moment it got there. "Let's get out of here. I'm probably grounded times fifty. How long have we been gone?"

"I don't know, but I'm not looking forward to hearing Grandpa's mouth...actually, this time, I think I won't mind," said Wendy.

Stephen lifted himself from the hard floor and carefully walked up the basement stairs, tapping his toe roughly on each stair to make sure they wouldn't cave. The last thing he needed was to be transported into some other world...again. When he found every stair to be stable, he yelled for Wendy to come up.

The lightbulb at the top of the stairwell still shined brightly without any flicker. Stephen looked behind himself to make sure Wendy was still there. He put his hand on the basement doorknob and twisted it. The door opened with a slow creak. Grandpa Lou, whom they expected would be awake by now, still slept peacefully in his rocking chair, swaying back and forth toward the basement door.

Stephen crept past him, signaling for Wendy to remain quiet. He felt jittery, like the time when he had eaten all of Matt's candy on Halloween. He carefully tiptoed to the front door and opened it. The sun shined on every lime-and-yellow-green-leafed tree. The streets were empty as usual with only the occasional bird stopping to plunge its beak into the wet soil. It had rained. Had it been raining when Stephen left? He couldn't remember. He wondered again how much time had passed. He looked at his house, plain and grayish like the rest of the Wally Heights houses. A feeling of relief passed over him.

"Should you get home?" Wendy whispered, standing behind Stephen. He stepped outside the door and motioned for Wendy to follow him out.

"Just one more thing," he said. "One more place."

"Ugh, you don't mean..."

"We gotta check," said Stephen. "We have to make sure the Hideaways are cured. I don't want anymore problems."

Wendy sighed, but nonetheless, followed Stephen to the McCallister house. Neither of them talked along the way. Instead, Stephen thought about Sir Edward Duke, about Mary, about the Hideaways watching him carefully as he walked to where they lived. He shook off a feeling of dread. Finding out about the Hideaways was more important than being afraid right now.

Before long, Stephen and Wendy stood in front of the McCallister house, squinting at the windows, searching for anything that watched them back.

"Can you see anything?" Wendy asked.

"Nothing," Stephen answered. He walked up to the house and peeked inside of the doorway, stepping on the large, rectangular board that he had knocked down when he originally explored the house. He hadn't looked back to check, but he assumed that Wendy had followed him.

"Hello?" Stephen called. He shook off the image of Wendy and him lying in the middle of the floor tied up. "Hello?" he called again.

No answer.

"Do you think they left?" asked Wendy.

"I certainly would," Stephen said, looking around him.

"It's probably technically not possible for humans to live here," said Wendy.

"Anything is possible," said Stephen. He searched the kitchen, finding only a few open cabinet doors with rotten wood. He walked toward the door and looked at the guitar propped up against a corner wall. No one played.

"I guess they're really gone," said Stephen.

"Geez, they could have at least said thank you," Wendy said.

"I think I'm okay with not getting a goodbye. Let's go."

But as they turned toward the doorway to walk home, they saw a tall man with big arms and a strong, wide chest standing in the doorway.

"Ahhh, look who's come back. Don't you

have work to do? After all, the night will be upon us soon," the sneering man said.

"Work to do? What are you talki—" Stephen stopped mid-sentence as soon as he realized it. The golden hair down to his shoulders, the tight-fitting black pants with the loose white shirt, those eyes.

Wendy stole Stephen's thoughts. "Ronald?" she asked in amazement.

"Yes? Have you come to refuse to do what I've asked of you?" Ronald asked as he walked toward the children. His steps were deliberate and calculated.

"It's over; we did it already," Stephen said hurriedly.

Ronald's expression didn't change. He clenched his strong square jaw and smirked. Something about his face looked dangerous.

"It's true!" Wendy chimed in. "We can see you. All of you. He's telling the truth!"

Ronald's smirk widened as he continued to walk. Stephen walked backwards, keeping a close eye on Ronald.

"You don't have to watch us anymore and no one has to get hurt. We made the wish. It's all over!" Stephen exclaimed.

"Do you think I'm a fool?" Ronald asked, slowing down the pace of his steps. He stared at Stephen and Wendy intently.

"No, it's true! You look like one of us now," said Stephen. Ronald seemed unmoved.

"You're wearing black pants and a white shirt!" Stephen yelled. He dug the tips of his nails into his palms, hoping Ronald believed him.

"It's not the most complicated of outfits to guess," Ronald said.

"Uh ummm...your hair is blonde and your lips are really pink and you're really strong," said Wendy.

"Something you could've easily seen in the fog vision that I gave you." By now, Ronald was just inches from the children. Close enough to grab them.

"What do *I* look like?" Stephen heard an older, familiar man's voice ask. A gray-haired man with heavy creases in his face walked through the door and toward Stephen. Those had to be the narrow gray eyes that were always around Ronald. The older man hadn't been in Ronald's story of how the Hideaways came to be. This, Stephen had decided, would probably be their last chance to prove that the Hideaway curse had been broken. But there was one problem. The old man was wearing nearly the exact same thing as Ronald. Stephen searched frantically for something to distinguish him from Ronald. Something to make the Hideaways realize that he wasn't lying.

The old man studied Wendy and Stephen, perhaps seeing the panic in their faces. "You both make the face that I'm making at the same time. No looking at each other. Agreed?" he said.

"Deal," said Stephen. Wendy nodded in agreement.

Stephen opened his hands and raised them to the top of his head like he was making deer antlers—just as the old man was doing. He wiggled all ten fingers and stuck his tongue out at the same time. He didn't dare look over at Wendy.

Still following the old man, Stephen put his hands down at his side and jumped three times. He could tell by the thumping sound that Wendy was also following. Stephen put his right foot out in front of him and rotated it, and then made a kicking motion.

"Heavens," the old man said.

"Do you mean...?" Ronald started to ask.

"They *can* see us. They've done it," said the old man. The creases in his face straightened a little, his jaw hanging in amazement.

"You've done it?" Ronald asked, turning to the children.

"That's what we've been trying to tell you," said Stephen.

"*Now* will you quit watching us?" asked Wendy.

"Why, this is amazing!" Ronald said, embracing the children. His shirt felt smooth and silk-like against Stephen's face, but it smelled like an old stuffy house with cats.

Ronald had perhaps forgotten his strength as a human and hugged Stephen just a little too hard. Stephen started to turn red from the embrace.

"How did you do it? Well, I guess none of it matters. You've done it! Why, it all makes sense. No wonder. We could no longer sit in this house anymore. The smell, the dust, the mold. It all bothers us now, but never did we think...you've done it!" Ronald yelled, embracing the children harder. Stephen coughed a little, trying to regain his wind. Ronald's excitement both frightened him and relieved him. Stephen didn't really want to be near him at all, but he dared not run.

"You've done it? Papa, he's done it?" A little girl, with small brown eyes and blonde pigtails, stood by the door. She hugged the old man's leg excitedly.

"Yes, my dear, they've done it," Ronald answered, stepping back and looking at the children.

"I suppose it's time for a move now. Thank you. Really. Thank you for all you've done."

"Were you really going to go after us and our families if we didn't help you?" Stephen asked curiously.

"That is for me to know and for you to

never find out," said Ronald with a smile on his face.

"So this is it, right? No more watching, no more threats? I mean, you're going away now that we've done our part, right?" asked Stephen.

"I guess this *is* the end," Ronald said, looking at the children. He extended his hand to Stephen. "Take care. Stay brave," he said.

"Thanks," Stephen said. He didn't take Ronald's hand. Instead, he looked toward the doorway of the McCallister house, itching to run out.

"Stay wise," Ronald said, shaking his head at Wendy.

Wendy didn't answer. "No more hanging around us? You'll leave us alone, right?" she finally said.

Stephen kept his eyes on the doorway, prepared to walk out of the McCallister house for the last time—that is, until the next town meeting. And there, nothing would watch him.

Ronald smiled and looked at his family. The old man smiled back and winked. He turned to Wendy with half of the smile that he had had before. "Something like that," Ronald answered.

CHAPTER 27

While part of Stephen was grateful that the Hideaways would be gone, he couldn't help but wonder what Ronald's final words had meant: *"Something like that."* He had been eager to get home, so he hadn't thought much of it at the time, but now on the walk home, those words echoed in Stephen's mind. *Something like that. Something like that.*

"What do you think Ronald meant by his answer?" Stephen asked Wendy, filling the silence between them.

"Which answer?" asked Wendy.

"Something like that," Stephen said, mimicking Ronald's eloquent voice.

Wendy giggled. "I don't know. Maybe he just meant he would never forget us."

"Yeah...maybe."

"That's what I thought, anyway. We held up our end of the bargain," Wendy said, sensing Stephen's hesitance.

Stephen no longer wanted to talk about

being watched. He had done everything that he was supposed to. Being watched was in the past.

"Hey, I don't know if I ever *really* thanked you. Thanks again for helping me back there with the wolves," he said.

"No problem," Wendy said proudly.

"You know, science is actually pretty cool. I mean, you know, it was cool how you knew the wolves would chase the ball and all," said Stephen.

"That's just mild science stuff. For Christmas, I got these roach specimens that I look at under a microscope. I can look at their heads, or legs, and probably even their guts."

"Cool!" Stephen shouted. For a girl, Wendy might not have been so bad after all.

"Wanna see?" Wendy asked, seeming hopeful. "I got them for a gift, but sometimes it's no fun looking at them alone."

"Cool, yeah. Just let me ask my parents. If I'm not grounded for a bajillion more years, I'll come over. Stay tuned," Stephen said, running up to his front door.

He took a deep breath and rang the doorbell. His mouth felt dry, and his throat was parched like it'd hurt him if he spoke. What would his dad say to him? What would his mom say? He braced himself.

"What do you want?" Stephen heard Matt's voice say as he opened up the door. This was the first time that he was genuinely happy to see Matt. He fought back the urge to wrap his arms around his older brother.

"Not you. Where's Mom and Dad?" Stephen asked, smiling.

"Gone. They went to their bowling league. Don't you have something better to do? Why aren't you out?"

"Out? I've been out...haven't I?" Stephen asked. Just how long had he been gone, again?

"You finally get a free pass to go out when you're on punishment and you only hang out for one measly hour. What a dweeb," said Matt.

"One hour?" Stephen said, puzzled. "Is that all?"

"What happened to your pants?" Matt asked, looking down at the rip. "Aren't those the pants that Mom loves? She's going to freak! This is the second pair that you've ripped."

"I'm going over Wendy's house. Bye," Stephen said, smiling as he rushed away from the front door and toward Wendy, who stood on the sidewalk waiting for him.

But as Stephen walked away from his door and toward Wendy, he felt something familiar. The trees seemed to be reaching for him, their shadows covering him completely. The sun, which felt comforting and warming minutes earlier, zeroed in on him, shined on him, watched him just long enough to know where he was going next. He looked to every house's window and door, but he could see nothing. Yet, still, he felt something watching him.

CHAPTER 28

Wendy lay in her bed, facing the rows of stuffed animals in her closet that peacefully watched over her. Her bedsheets felt like smooth, warm cotton against her dry skin. The nighttime was Wendy's favorite part of the day. Everything was so still. It allowed her time to think. After all, today had been quite a day. She had saved an entire town that was hundreds of years old, and in the process, she had even made a new friend. Stephen Humphries wasn't so bad—for a boy, that is. She tucked the silver locket that Mary had given her underneath her pillow and clapped her hands to shut the lights off.

But then, she heard something unusual that sounded like a bump. She froze, remembering the time that the Hideaways had come to visit her in her room. She suddenly felt alert. Even the low swish of her ceiling fan sounded louder now. Had the Hideaways come to visit her again? No. It couldn't be.

The Hideaways' curse had been cured. There was no reason for them to follow her now. No more Hideaways and no more eyes.

She turned around, preparing herself in case two curious eyes stared back at her. She threw her hand over her mouth to muffle her scream, but she soon saw there was no need. She could see no whites of eyes staring at her in the dark.

Wendy laughed at herself. The day—more specifically, the lingering sets of eyes she had encountered—had taken its toll on her. But it was all over now. Yes. No more Hideaways. No more eyes.

And then, another bump. She had heard it even more clearly than the first one. Something had tapped lightly against her bedroom door. She stared at the block of light shining through the bottom of the door. She was sure of it now. The sound had definitely been coming from the outside.

She swung her long legs over the side of the bed. *I'm brave. I can handle this,* Wendy thought, remembering Mary's words: '*You are more brave than you think.*' She shivered when her feet hit the cold, wooden floor. Who could be at her door? She could have sworn Grandpa was asleep, but maybe she was wrong. Maybe he had stayed up late for a particular reason. Maybe he—

She heard it again—an even louder bump

that made her jump. She turned the doorknob and yanked the door open.

Her fear turned into relief when she saw Grandpa Lou, hunched over in the hallway, moving a set of cardboard boxes. He shuffled through them anxiously, tossing a few to the side toward Wendy's door. It was something he did every once in a while when he wanted to reminisce and remember all of the women who wrote him during the war. He either kept forgetting where he put the letters or he never found them.

"Grandpa, I think you hit my door," Wendy said, holding her chest. Grandpa Lou didn't seem bothered. He continued to shuffle through the brown boxes in the hallway as if he hadn't even heard her.

"Sorry," he managed to mumble eventually.

"Goodnight, Grandpa," Wendy said, softly closing her door. She shook her head as she climbed underneath the sheets. She felt downright silly. How had she not guessed the sound was Grandpa? He was the only other person in the house.

She climbed beneath her soft, velvet-like sheets and closed her eyes, ready to drift off to wherever her dreams took her.

"Psst!" Wendy heard a soft, high-pitched sound. She flicked her eyes open and sat up, pulling her sheets to her chin.

"Hey! You!" There the noise was again.

This time, there was no mistaking what she heard. It was a voice. One other than her own and Grandpa Lou's.

"Who's there?" Wendy asked, frightened. Her voice trembled, though she wished it didn't.

"Hey! Down here!"

Wendy carefully leaned over the foot of her bed. She shrieked and scooted back. A small man who looked to be less than a foot tall, maybe even less than five inches, looked up at her. Large, furry and pointy rat ears sat on top of his head. She had been rather caught off guard by how normal the man appeared, with the exception of his size and his ears, of course.

"Hey, calm it down, will you? Someone will hear you," the man said in his squeaky voice. When she looked closer, she could see a smaller version of the man standing beside him.

"Get out of my room! Who are you? How'd you get here?" she demanded as she scooted back toward her headboard. She clapped her hands to turn on the lights.

"Look, I realize you may be slightly frightened. Just calm down. Please. We need you."

"You need me?" Wendy exclaimed. She grabbed her covers tighter.

"Yes." The man paused. He held both

palms out to Wendy. "Don't be afraid..." He waved his hand toward Wendy's bed and then the closet.

A long man, who looked so flattened that he appeared to be a sheet of paper, emerged from beneath her bed. Wendy screamed as she fell off the other end of the bed near the closet and thumped on the floor.

Perhaps she had begun to run out of good luck. Out of the closet emerged a giant, human-sized worm that seemed to have no end. It looked at Wendy shyly and bowed its head when she made eye contact. Slowly, it began to slide toward the foot of Wendy's bed.

Wendy grew dizzy with fear. She could hardly breathe. Her hands shook as she lifted them to her face. Both the worm and the paper-thin man had walked over to join the small, rat-eared man.

"You see," the rat-eared man started. "Ummm, well...we heard that you helped the Hideaways. You know, with reversing the wishmaster's curse."

Wendy grew hot with anticipation and fear. She started to itch all over. She knew what question was to come next. It was the very one that had given her nightmares for months before she cured the Hideaway curse. The very question that drove her to enter another world and fight a balding wishmaster with wishes.

"Our wishmasters haven't been so kind, either," said the rat man.

"Can you help us?" the deep-voiced, paper-thin man said.

Wendy looked past the foot of her bed and at her bedroom door, wondering if Grandpa had heard her scream. Rat man, paper man, the worm, and the smiling stuffed animals all watched her, waiting for an answer.

AUTHOR BIO

 Kendra Hadnott is an author, educator, and blogger (www. litlikeme.com). Her work has been featured in *Windows Fine Arts* magazine, *Mosaic* magazine, and most recently, in the Chicago Center for Literature and Photography's *Chicago After Dark* anthology.

Here's her most famed advice to aspiring authors and artists in general: "Believe in yourself and make your own way. Everybody won't understand or agree with your decision to pursue your passion. In those instances, don't do anything to prove people wrong. Do everything to prove yourself right."

To connect with Kendra or learn more about her, visit www.kendrahadnott.com, along with her Facebook page under "Author Kendra Hadnott."